AUGUST SUNSETS

The Vineyard Sunset Series Book Three

KATIE WINTERS

CHAPTER 1

THE WIND RIPPLED OFF THE VINEYARD SOUND AND SWEPT across Lola's face. She eyed the horizon, her fingers placed delicately on her MacBook and her mind abuzz. Far in the distance, a large vessel trickled across the water. Somewhere just beyond was a sailboat, probably one that belonged to someone from the neighboring Naushon Island. Although it was only eight in the morning, the islanders of the eastern portion of New England were early risers and, accordingly, early sailors. Some said the water, the crisp air, the light was at its most pristine before nine. After that, the day was considered a wash.

Lola, whose mind was always rife with imagination, forced her thoughts to return to the topic at hand. In this case, it was the story due for her Boston-based editor, Colin, before the day's end. It was a write-up of one of the trendiest new brunch spots in Boston. The week before, Lola had left the Vineyard and feasted on delicacies like eggs benedict and fluffy crepes and honey glazed bacon, while sipping down breakfast cocktails and interviewing the chef and owner, a married couple team.

Sometimes, being a journalist wasn't so bad. The perks were really something to write home about, that was for sure.

The thing that strikes me most about Boston's newest top brunch offering is the friendliness of its owners, Brad and Paula Carroway, who both grew up in the Boston suburbs and wanted to bring their love of interior design, community, and damn good food together in a single place.

Lola tilted her head at the words she'd drummed up, again lost in thought. She'd worked as a journalist since her early to mid-20s, having nabbed her first gig when Audrey had been around three and a half years old. In some ways, she missed those very early days. It had been a constant battle. She had always had to give herself two or three personal checks to ensure no crummy kid food had gotten on her new second-hand business clothes. She had worked nights and weekends and, admittedly, used her friends in Boston for babysitting a few times too many. She'd missed Audrey with a dull ache in her heart when she'd gone out on location, but she'd also known that every step she took deeper into the field of journalism was a step toward happiness for both herself and Audrey. When she'd gotten her first story in a major newspaper, Audrey had been seven, and they had celebrated with milkshakes at McDonald's. Audrey had been her best girl, the person she'd done everything for.

Shoot. Her mind had run away with itself again. She forced it back to brunch space and wrote poetics about the bright raspberry jam, the light that streamed in through the enormous windows, the way Paula spoke about Brad in this way like, he was the greatest thing that had ever happened to her. The way Brad had said the same.

Of course, during this particular part, Lola's heart burned. Was it jealousy? Want? She wasn't sure. She'd had such a long string of boyfriends—mostly artists, musicians, filmmakers, that sort of thing —all of whom had been monstrous in their own way. She'd kicked all of them to the curb, and held her chin high. Still, at thirty-eight, almost thirty-nine, it had begun to feel like maybe true love would never happen for her.

When she had mentioned this to Christine recently, of course, Christine had just shrugged and said, "Look what happened to me? I'm the crankiest person you know, and even I'm falling in love with Zach Walters. Of all people."

Lola was genuinely pleased at Christine's newfound happiness. It had been difficult for her, at first, to consider the idea that Christine might initially raise her grandchild; however, watching Christine as she began to prepare for it, already, made her heart light. Christine had asked Aunt Kerry to help her learn to knit (Christine! Knitting!), and she and Aunt Kerry had spent the better part of the previous afternoon on the back porch doing just that. Already, Christine had half a baby's bonnet knitted.

People could change.

Change was the only constant.

This particular morning, Lola was one of the only ones at home. This was irregular since, normally, the place was overflowing with Sheridan-related humans. Scott was nearly finished with the two extra bedrooms he had decided to build up on the side of the house, which would certainly help with lodging. That morning, however, he and Susan continued to sleep on at his place. Susan

3

had had another chemotherapy treatment two days before, and she expressed that she felt knocked out from that particular one and didn't have the strength to do much but lay in bed.

Audrey had decided to take the weekend to visit a few of her girlfriends back in Boston. There was a fresh lightness to her daughter, an eagerness to her eyes. Lola had caught her typing excitedly on her computer several times over the past week. When she had prodded her about it, Audrey had shrugged and said she was back to writing again. The morning sickness had calmed a tiny bit. Still, at only approximately two months pregnant, and certainly eating enough for two, Audrey's stomach remained flat. Metabolism was a wild thing.

Lola lifted her arms over her head and cracked her knuckles. Her heart bulged with happiness over the story she'd just written up; she knew her editor, Colin, would love it. He always said Lola was overly emotional, which made her writing a pleasure to read. Lola had always known this about herself. Wes always cited her as the daughter who'd cried the most. Heck, she even felt like crying now, just at the enormous weight of all the family drama they'd gone through since early June.

It had been one hell of a summer that was for sure. And it was still only the beginning of August.

What could happen next?

Lola penned an email to her editor and sent off the article. It was now only eight-thirty. She decided to head inside to say hello to her father since she was the only one around and he always liked the company while he did his puzzles or wrote in his little notebook.

"Hey, Dad!" she called, pulling open the screen door.

The table held a half-finished puzzle, which featured an old sailboat latched to a dock. A half-drunk cup of coffee sat beside the box, along with a nibbled croissant. Wes Sheridan didn't sit in front of any of it. Only Felix, the cat Christine had brought back from New York, stepped out from beneath the table and let out a meow, followed by a yawn.

"Dad?"

She assumed he was just upstairs. She stepped toward the entry to the staircase and called up, but received no answer.

Now, her heart beat quickly in her throat. "Dad?" She scampered up the steps to find his bedroom empty, the bed all made up and the laundry folded on the edge, something she had dropped off earlier that morning.

Lola was the only sister home. She was the one meant to remain at the homestead and watch over their father, who, since his diagnosis, wasn't allowed to remain at home alone any longer. He had nearly burned the place down in early June, which was the original reason Susan had called them all back to the island.

Had Lola really let him leave the house alone?

She had heard this was a thing with dementia patients: that frequently, they got confused and wandered off. Panicked, she grabbed her keys and phone and raced outside. Luckily, the only car that had been parked in the driveway remained there, which meant that Wes had gone off on foot. She rushed around the house, eyeing the edge of the water and the forest.

"DAD?" Her voice echoed across the waves.

Her mind went to a dark place as she searched. She imagined herself explaining the situation to her sisters, that she had lost track of time while writing on the porch, returned to the kitchen and found him gone. Susan would give her that look—one she recognized from early childhood. It was a look that proved just how disappointed she was in you. Christine and Lola had always joked that this look was just something genetic, passed down to Susan and only Susan because she was the oldest and most responsible.

Where could he have gone to?

Lola paused, gasping and gripping her knees. Suddenly, her phone began to buzz. She blinked at the name. AUDREY.

"Hello?"

"Mom, hey. What's up?"

"Um. Nothing, honey, how are you?" She lifted herself and placed her hand on her hips. She tried to live in the beauty of her daughter's voice while praying to God above that she would find her father in a few minutes. Maybe he was just down the trail, headed toward the Inn? Maybe he'd gotten it in his head that he was needed at work?

"You sound weird," Audrey said.

"No, I don't."

"Whatever," Audrey returned. "I just wanted to tell you something I discovered today. I have a new pregnancy craving."

Lola swallowed a lump in her throat. She hunkered toward the edge of the forest but kept her voice bright. "What's that, honey?"

"It's Fig Newtons," Audrey continued. "I can't get enough of them. I ate a whole sleeve last night with Rory. Seriously, I'm going to have to stockpile them when I get back. The doctor said I need to start gaining a little bit more weight, right? Maybe this is the way."

Lola paused at the entry to the woods and peered in, her eyebrows low.

"Mom? Are you even listening to me?" Audrey asked.

"Yes, Audrey. Fig Newtons. Sorry, I guess I never bought those when you were growing up."

"You had all those organic food kicks, I guess," Audrey returned. "Not now that we live with Aunt Christine. All those croissants."

"You could say we've transitioned to being a carb family now, I guess," Lola said.

Her heart pumping, she stepped into the woods. She thought she spotted something deep within, a kind of deep red coloring that very well could have been her father's coat. Then again, it could have been a bush or a bird or a bit of trash left out by a littering tourist.

"Well, it's been really marvelous being here," Audrey continued. "I got up the courage to call the editor of the Penn State paper yesterday. He says it's no trouble if I keep writing some articles from afar, just to keep my portfolio up. He says he'll welcome me back next year. He also says it's a pretty wild thing, a girl at a university like Penn State actually going through with a pregnancy like this. He wants me to write a think-piece about it."

"That's fantastic news, Audrey," Lola murmured.

She'd closed in on the dark red color and confirmed it: it was Wes Sheridan's spring and fall coat. He stood in the center of a small clearing; his binoculars lifted over his eyes and his chin high. Lola followed the direction of the binoculars to see a woodpecker sitting on top of a branch, digging his beak into the wood.

"What's that sound, Mom? Where are you?" Audrey asked.

"I'm going to have to call you back, baby," Lola said. "I have to talk to Grandpa about something for a second. Love you. And thank you for the news. About the paper and, of course, about the Fig Newtons."

Audrey giggled. "Any time, Mom. Love you, too. And, miss you, as weird as that sounds. It's only been a few days."

"I know. Me too."

Lola hung up the phone and walked delicately toward her father. She didn't want to scare him; she also knew that it was beside the point to tell him how upset she was that he had run off like that without letting anyone know.

Softly, she murmured, "Dad?"

At this, Wes whipped around. His binoculars fell to his chest. He looked at her; his face marred with confusion and then rubbed his eyes.

"Anna, there you are," he finally said. "I wanted to show you this woodpecker. The coloring is something I've never seen before. It's so beautiful. Where have you been?"

CHAPTER 2

LOLA KNEW THAT OF ALL THE SHERIDAN SISTERS, SHE LOOKED the most like their dead mother, Anna. Add to that the fact that she was thirty-eight, the same age her mother had been at the time of her death, and she didn't blame her father for his confusion. Heck, even she started when she saw pictures of her mother sometimes. The resemblance was uncanny and she kept it that way, ensuring her hair remained long, flowing down her back.

"It's not Anna, Dad. It's me. It's Lola," she said softly.

For a moment, Wes's eyes stirred with confusion again. His hand stroked his stomach, and he tilted his head. "Right. Well, regardless—you really must see this woodpecker. Whoever you are." At this, he winked, as though he wanted to be in on the joke about his declining mental health.

Naturally, Lola didn't laugh.

She did step toward him and accept the binoculars, so that she could peer up at the bird, at its gorgeous yet peculiar red markings.

Her father placed his hand on her shoulder and said, "I love it out here. Just me and the birds and the squirrels. Glad to share it with you."

Lola dropped the binoculars onto her chest. Her heart stirred with panic, fear, and sadness, and she surged toward him and hugged him tightly. He seemed both shocked and open to it, and he slid his hand down her back and said, "What a wonderful way to start the day."

Lola sniffled and drew her head back. She was reminded of a long-lost time when Audrey had taken her rollerblades out to the parking lot beneath their apartment building. Lola had worked in the living room, with a full view of the parking lot. After a few minutes, however, she had blinked up to see that the parking lot was empty. When she'd scampered down, Audrey was nowhere to be found.

Eventually, she had found her on the other side of the building, trying to con an ice cream truck driver to give her a free cone.

This was the way of Audrey.

Heck, maybe it was just the way of the Sheridan clan.

"Why don't we go inside? I can cook us breakfast," Lola said. She snaked her arm through her father's and leaned her head against his chest.

"Breakfast? Wow, what a treat," her father said.

"We can head back out to watch birds later if you want," Lola returned. "I just finished my article for the day, so I have the rest of it free."

"Must be nice, being a freelancer," he said. "Making your own schedule like that."

"I guess you were shackled to the Inn for all those years," Lola said. "Must have been exhausting."

"It was like constantly having a toddler," Wes said with a laugh.

"A toddler like me, or a toddler like Susan?" Lola asked.

"I think you know the answer to that," Wes returned. "Susan could have done her own taxes at the age of four."

"Fair enough."

Back at the house, Lola brewed up a fresh pot of coffee, and Wes returned to his puzzle. She turned on the old radio and began to heat some oil and slice some potatoes. As the potatoes began to fry, she grabbed her phone and swiftly shot toward the back mudroom, where she knew she could chat with someone in peace.

Immediately, she dialed the doctor.

"Hey. Thank you so much for taking my call," she began.

"Not a problem, Lola. Anything for the Sheridans," Doctor Miller said. "What's up?"

"Well, my dad kind of ran away this morning. I found him, but he was a little bit confused. And it's not like him to just leave without telling me," Lola said. "I wondered if you think I should bring him in for a check-up?"

Doctor Miller clucked his tongue. Lola remembered this very tick from when he'd grown up with Christine and Susan. He had been a little bit older than her, but she'd seen him around.

"I guess it stands to reason that he would do something like that. He's reaching that stage of the illness, I suppose. If he's not injured and feeling okay now, then I guess it would only alarm him to bring him in," Doctor Miller said. "All we can do during these stages is make sure he's comfortable and happy and that his mind is occupied."

"I guess it's up to me to keep better watch on him, then," Lola said with a sigh.

"I'm afraid so. I'm sorry this happened. It must have given you a good scare."

"That's putting it lightly."

They hung up. Lola went back to stir the potatoes and check on Wes again, then returned to the mudroom to dial Christine and Susan. Neither of them answered the phone. Lola breathed a sigh of relief. She would tell them what happened another time. Heck, maybe she wouldn't tell them at all.

They had avoided disaster before. All they could do was keep going.

Lola fried up some eggs and placed them, glowing yolks and all, across the old china that her mother had picked out. She then added the crispy potatoes and dotted their plates on the porch picnic table. The breakfast table had long since been designated as the puzzle table. Nobody dared touch it or eat there.

Out on the picnic table, they both inhaled the fresh morning air and ate heartily. Lola told her father a bit about her article about the brunch place in Boston and also about her editor back there, Colin.

"We used to work together at a different paper, around ten years ago," she said. "And he's a really great guy. One of the best I've met. He's a huge champion of my writing, and he gives me a leg up all the time. I don't know where I would be without him," Lola explained.

"What a good friend to have," Wes said. He arched his brow and chewed his potatoes contemplatively. "I don't suppose you ever considered him as a potential, you know—date?"

Lola stifled a laugh as she peered at her father. Was it possible that he was better at reading people than she'd always thought? Since she felt calmness— a stillness after the panic earlier that morning, she decided to just come out with the truth.

"We actually dated briefly about ten years ago," she said. "When we worked at that same newspaper. It went okay. I mean, I was, what? Twenty-eight at the time? And he was only thirty, and he wasn't really sure about the whole, me having a kid aged nine, thing. He didn't meet Audrey till years later when we rekindled our friendship."

"Interesting," Wes said. "Again, it's remarkable for me to hear stories about my girls' lives. All I ever knew was my high school sweetheart. All I ever knew was this island."

"I think you might have struck gold," Lola said with a laugh. "They always say that happiness is right in front of you if only you look for it."

"Well, that's certainly true for me at the moment," Wes returned, beaming at her.

"Dad..."

"I'm not talking about you. I'm talking about the potatoes," Wes said with a wink.

How could he still have such a sense of humor? Lola marveled at it and shook her head, a huge smile snaking from ear to ear.

That moment, they heard tires creak across the stones in the driveway. Lola yanked around to watch as Scott led Susan in through the back door. They were bleary and shadowed, with the screen door between them. Lola lifted her hand in greeting.

"What smells so good?" Susan asked. Her voice wavered a bit, proof of her fatigue. Still, when she appeared in the crack of the door, she grinned down at Lola and Wes with a clear smile.

"There are plenty more potatoes if you want to heat them up," Lola affirmed.

"Ah, maybe Scott is interested. Unfortunately, I can hardly keep anything down," Susan said. She slipped onto the bench beside Lola and unraveled her pretty pink scarf and placed her hand across her bald head. "I wondered if you wanted to go check out wigs with me later today."

Scott appeared in the screen door next, having already filled up his plate with potatoes. "She has dreams of being a redhead, apparently."

"I don't see why I shouldn't experiment," Susan said. "All my life, I've looked about the same. Now's the time." She leaned toward Lola, her eyes twinkling conspiratorially. "I'm thinking, like, Julianne Moore. That kind of red."

"Oh. Lush," Lola said. "I fully support this decision."

Before Lola sped off to go wig shopping with Susan, she turned her eyes toward her father and said, "I think we have something to do together, first."

"You didn't forget," Wes said. He saluted her. "I'll grab my binoculars."

It was agreed that Susan and Lola would depart just after one-thirty, which gave them plenty of time to bird watch. Wes pointed out a whole host of dramatically colored birds, all with different sounds and behaviors. Lola was surprised how much pleasure she took in it. Once, she spotted one her father missed, and she ripped her finger through the air and called a bit too loudly, "There it is! Wow. Look at the wingspan!"

If Audrey had seen her, she would have scoffed something like, *Who are you, and what have you done with my mother?*

Just before Susan and Lola headed off, Christine arrived home from the bistro. She ruffled her long hair and gave them an exasperated smile. "The lunch rush at the beginning was insane, so I told Zach I would help until we found a gap for me to leave."

Susan explained the plan, and Christine readily agreed to head off with them. There was a wig shop in Edgartown, not too far from Zach's place. Lola leaped into the driver's seat, watching as Susan gingerly placed herself in the passenger. Christine leaped into the back, buzzing with adrenaline from her long workday. Still, Lola knew she loved the restaurant rush. It gave her purpose, the same way writing an article did for Lola.

Once at the wig shop, Lola, Christine, and Susan wandered the aisles, hunting for the perfect wig. Of course, they started out jokingly, tapping a purple and then a blue wig onto Susan's head. She glanced at herself in the mirror and muttered, "Oh my. I look like a weird pop star."

"I kind of like it," Christine said. "You look like you're a woman who knows what she wants."

"I *am* a woman who knows what she wants. What I want is to be a hot redhead," Susan returned, removing the shiny, blue wig.

She tried out several: a golden-red, then a deeper one that seemed closer to her actual hair color. She arched her brow, then tried on a black one, joking that she might enter a "gothic" phase now.

"I'm always deathly pale now, anyway," she said. "Maybe it's time."

Ultimately, she chose the dark red wig, which flowed past her shoulders and looked fresh and bouncy. The owner of the shop showed her how to put it on properly, and she walked out of the place with a fresh 'do—beaming at her sisters.

"Why haven't I changed my look all these years?" she asked. "How boring of me."

Lola and Christine exchanged glances. Both wore grins, but their eyes were somber. Although this activity was masked as fun, it was edged with sadness. They were still only a bit into Susan's chemotherapy treatment, and there was really no telling what would happen next. All they could do was hope.

CHAPTER 3

Several days later, Christine and Lola perched at the front edge of the car, little ice cream cups in hand. Their eyes scanned the water, hunting for the first sign of the ferry boat that Audrey had hopped on en route from her little trip to Boston. Lola smeared the very edge of her spoon across the icy strawberry delight and dabbed the cream across her tongue. Pangs of delightful flavor shot through her.

"Why don't we eat more ice cream?" she asked. "This is fantastic."

"I agree. Let's make a note of it." Christine chuckled. "By the way, Zach said the cutest thing last night."

"What's that?"

"He said that he wants to build the baby a cradle—with his bare hands. I never imagined I'd be with such a capable man," Christine said.

Lola gave Christine a genuine smile. There it was again: that light behind Christine's eyes. The joy of a future baby, someone to care for, to live for. Christine had told Lola and Susan about the tremendous horrors that had plagued Zach's life, which made his excitement for Audrey's baby all the more special. Lola remembered that old expression: *It takes a village to raise a child.* She thought, in this case, it couldn't have been truer.

"Are you nervous about it at all?" Lola asked.

"Of course," Christine returned. "I'm probably going to read every single mommy blog between now and then. I've already listened to like five different podcasts about it. I'm not normally the type of woman to fully prepare for everything. I like to just dive in, you know? But with something this special, I need to be ready."

Out in the distance on the water, a sailboat flowed past. Its sails whipped around dramatically, like cream-colored wings. Lola paused, forgetting even her ice cream.

"Have you talked to Tommy since the hospital?" Christine asked suddenly.

Lola was surprised that Christine brought this up now. The accident had occurred during the Round-the-Island Race a little over a week before. Lola had written the article about Tommy Gasbarro, the ex-stepson of Stan Ellis and she had been genuinely mesmerized with his gruff exterior, his sailing abilities, his captivating eyes, and of course, the fact that he had actually met their mother, Anna when he'd been a teenager visiting Stan on the island. When he had crashed his boat at the tail-end of the race, Lola had forced Christine to the hospital to check on him. When Tommy had awoken, he'd been a bit too groggy to speak. She'd taken his hand and told him that everything was all right; he would be okay. In his haze, he had called her an angel.

"No. Not at all," Lola answered. "Most of the time I was there with him, he slept. I felt bad to take up the space by his bed when I knew Stan wanted it. And it's not like I could pester Tommy with questions right after the accident. I'm curious, but I'm not a monster."

"Fair enough," Christine said. She arched her brow and slid her spoon through her chocolate mousse ice cream. "Still, you seemed into him. Weren't you?"

"There's the boat!" Lola cried. Her heart leaped into her throat. There, coming out of the strange fog of the August afternoon, was the traditional ferry boat that took tourists from Falmouth to Martha's Vineyard.

"Well, that is one way to avoid the question," Christine said, heaving a sigh.

"There's no answer to it. It was all business. That's all," Lola returned.

Christine collected their empty cups and disposed of them in the nearby trash can. They then snuck up toward the edge of the dock, where they could see the first glimpse of Audrey atop the boat. To their surprise, someone who could have been Audrey's twin stood beside her, grinning and waving madly.

"Amanda!" Lola and Christine cried in unison.

When Amanda and Audrey hopped off the boat, Christine and Lola showered them in hugs and kisses.

"You sneaky girl," Christine said to Amanda. "Your mom is going to lose it."

Amanda blushed. "I know she's been extra tired lately. I just wanted to come out and check on her."

"She's tired, but she's also more fashionable than ever," Lola affirmed.

"What do you mean?" Amanda asked.

"You'll see," Lola said with a wink.

Lola and Christine helped the girls with their bags, then slipped back into the car. Audrey and Amanda talked excitedly about this, their "secret scheme," and told Christine and Lola that Audrey had even gone to Newark for a day to meet Amanda's fiancé, Chris.

"I guess we're really becoming a family now," Lola joked as they entered the driveway.

Scott and Zach were toward the side of the main house, both shirtless and working on the last of the added on rooms. Christine leaped out of the car the second Lola turned off the engine and rushed toward Zach, wrapping her arms around him and dotting a kiss on his back.

Amanda was mesmerized. "I can't believe how quickly those rooms went up!"

"Scott has worked tirelessly," Lola said. "He knew we needed the extra space, said he would do it, and kept to his word. Imagine that."

"He's one of a kind in the male world," Audrey said, laughing.

Lola entered the house just after Amanda. They found Susan stretched out on the couch, the hair of her red wig splayed out on all sides of her face and across a bright white pillow. She looked beautiful, like a queen. Amanda shrieked.

"Mom! You look beautiful!"

Susan's grin was infectious. She swept her arm out to the side and gestured for her to come hug her. "You didn't tell me you were coming back to the Vineyard!"

"Aren't I allowed to surprise you?" Amanda asked.

"No. Who told you that you could do that?" Susan returned.

Susan lifted herself gingerly from the couch and reached down beneath the coffee table to bring out several interior design magazines. "I have been thinking all day about how we should decorate the bedrooms, now that they're nearly finished."

"That sounds like fun!" Christine said.

"Mom has loads of interesting decorations up in the attic," Lola affirmed.

"I thought of that, too," Susan said. "Stuff Dad put away over the years. And I thought we should paint one of the rooms a lilac color. Mom's favorite."

"That goes without saying!" Christine said.

"Scott agreed to bring over some beds from the Inn, some spare ones we keep in storage," Susan continued. "He said we'll be able to have people sleeping in there possibly tonight. Amanda, I always said you had decent timing, but this takes the cake."

"Ha. I try," Amanda said, smiling at her mother.

Later that afternoon, Susan said she had enough energy to hit up a few home improvement stores on the island to buy paint and other supplies to start the design of the new bedrooms. Lola, Audrey, Christine, Susan, and Amanda all piled into the car and had a blast at the store, inspecting paint colors and considering wallpaper and asking the big questions, like, carpet or hardwood or laminate? How would they light the rooms, since it would still be another few days before Scott could route the electricity? What curtains should they choose?

Time went by swiftly. Before long, all five Sheridan women were famished and ready to return home. They loaded up the supplies they had bought, then stopped at the grocery store to buy groceries for dinner. They decided on eggplant parmesan since Audrey suggested if she saw another burger that week, she might scream.

Back at the house, Wes, Zach, and Scott sat out on the picnic table, each nursing a beer. Wes was in the middle of an old story about his youth, talking about how the island had had a long-standing history of deafness. "It was a genetic thing," he told them. "Although back then, nobody really knew that so much. It was just considered a Martha's Vineyard trait."

"Fascinating," Zach said. "I can't imagine that. Probably a lot more people knew sign language."

"Yes, indeed," Wes affirmed. "In fact, my mother's grandmother was deaf, so my mother knew a bit."

"Wow. I didn't know it was a family thing," Christine said as they walked out onto the porch.

"Yes, indeed," Wes said. "I thanked my lucky stars that none of you girls were deaf. However, I have to think that even deafness is a kind of gift. Apparently, my great-grandmother could paint the most beautiful pictures. I asked my mother where these paintings ended up, and she said many of them were lost in a fire, years ago. Such a regret."

Again, Lola and Christine locked eyes, amazed at the things their father still remembered.

Back inside, Lola and Christine began to prepare dinner, while Susan and Audrey collapsed on the couch together. Amanda crossed her legs in the center of the living room, poring over another wedding magazine and speaking again about venues and flowers with her mother. She'd taken a liking to their cousin, Charlotte, and her daughter, Rachel, who ran an event planning company and had informed them of countless options on Martha's Vineyard for the following summer.

Again, Lola felt fear rise up from her stomach. All this talk of what would be, what would happen next. The certainty was overwhelming.

How could they possibly know that Susan would make it out of this?

In the two new bedrooms, Scott and Zach prepared the two new queen-sized beds while the dinner cooked. The women listened to them grunt and argue, albeit mildly, about what steps to do next.

"Are those two strong and able men I hear?" Susan joked, calling out.

"Two strong and able men about to kill each other, I think," Audrey affirmed.

"No, murdering!" Lola said. "At least, not before dinner."

Zach emerged from one of the bedrooms, slapping his palms together. He dotted a kiss on Christine's forehead as she continued to prepare the eggplant parmesan.

"A funny thing, having you in charge of the kitchen around here," he joked.

"Does it bother you to have a woman in charge?" Christine asked, arching an eyebrow.

"It's totally thrown off my game," Zach said with a wink.

"Figures. Fragile male ego, over here!" Audrey said with a smirk.

"You want to help me put together this bed, Audrey?" Zach teased.

Audrey placed her hand over her stomach and said, "Excuse me. I'm putting all my energy into growing this baby, thank you very much."

"I guess she's got me there," Zach shrugged. "I can't grow a human."

"Damn right, you can't," Susan said, grinning wider.

Together, the ever-growing Sheridan clan sat outside on the back porch and ate large portions of eggplant parmesan and garlic bread. Lola opened two bottles of cabernet and poured small glasses for everyone who wanted it. Christine, to her surprise, abstained. It was obvious to everyone that she wanted to cut back on her drinking. Lola guessed this was because she hadn't been this happy in a long time and just didn't need the extra support.

That night, Lola and Christine prepared the new beds. It was decided that, at least for that night, Susan and Scott would share one of the rooms, Amanda and Audrey, the other, while Lola and Christine would take the upper rooms. Zach agreed, after a moment of humming and hawing, that he wanted to stay, too. Slowly, the entire Sheridan clan prepared for bed: stitching themselves into their bedclothes and brushing their teeth in one of the two bathrooms. By the time eleven o'clock hit, everyone retreated to their rooms, including Felix, the cat, who joined Wes in his. Lola kind of loved that Felix had adopted Wes as his greatest love. Wes needed him more than anyone else did.

For the first time in ages, Lola slept peacefully. She felt that finally, her family home was complete.

CHAPTER 4

AMANDA HEADED BACK TO NEWARK A FEW DAYS LATER, AFTER a fun-filled few days of wedding planning, cooking, and chit chat on the back porch. Lola was amazed at how upbeat Susan was throughout Amanda's time with them. When she remarked on this to Christine, she said one thing: "She would do anything for that girl." And it was true. Susan's love for Amanda was one of the brightest lights Lola had ever seen. The girls were remarkably the same. Lola even noticed similarities between Susan and Lola's relationship and Amanda and Audrey's relationship, since both girls were so much like their mothers. The only difference, Lola supposed, was that Audrey and Amanda seemed to hardly fight about anything. That was the thing about growing up with someone. You always found a reason to fight.

The day of Amanda's departure, Audrey had an ultrasound scheduled at the local clinic. At first, Audrey had been a bit cagey about the whole thing, clearly unsure if she wanted to invite Lola along. But since she was only nineteen, there was a glimmer of fear in her eyes. A few minutes before she planned to leave, she asked Lola if she minded tagging along. Of course, Lola was already dressed and prepared. She wouldn't have missed it for the world.

In the waiting room, Lola watched as Audrey flicked nervously through her phone. They were about fifteen minutes early, due to both of their nerves, and there wasn't much to say. Lola had a magazine on her lap, but she hardly glanced at it. She liked the weight of it there. It reminded her of more normal things.

Audrey lifted her phone to her mother. Her eyes were tentative, but her words had that same harder edge, proof of some kind of confidence she wanted to project to the world.

"I guess I never showed you the guy," Audrey said.

"Oh. Right."

It wasn't that Lola hadn't been curious about who the father was. Audrey had been really cagey about that, too—saying that he was just some other journalist based in Chicago, that she had thought he was more serious about her than he was, that he wanted nothing to do with the pregnancy.

Now, she blinked down at the face of her grandchild's father. His name was Max Gray, and he was handsome—just as good looking as Audrey's father had been, or maybe even more. In the photo, he stood at the edge of a sailboat with his black hair glowing gently in the breeze. His smile was stellar, the kind of thing reserved for toothbrush commercials.

"Phew," Lola said.

"I know, right?" Audrey said. She gave a tiny smile, then shrugged. "I guess if my baby looks even a little bit like him, then I've done okay for the world."

"Maybe he or she will make you millions in baby modeling," Lola returned.

"Ha. I would never!" Audrey said. "I guess it's up to Christine, though."

"Maybe she'll turn your baby into a mega child star," Lola joked. "The next Mary Kate Olsen."

Audrey groaned. "Don't joke about that, Mom. The Olsen twins are messed up enough as it is."

Lola followed Audrey into the technician's room and watched as she lifted up her shirt to find that flat belly. The technician squirted goop across it then smeared it around with the scanner; her face turned toward the screen above all of them.

"There he or she is," the technician said, giving Audrey a big smile. "Everything looks like it's right on schedule. You're just about two months along."

"Only seven more to go!" Audrey said ironically as she stared at the ceiling.

"I promise you. It'll feel like the longest journey of your life. But you'll miss it when it's over," the technician said. "What do you think, Mom?"

Lola realized that she spoke to her this time. She looked up, surprised to be included, and said, "Oh? Yes. It's weird the things you miss. Not the swelling ankles, no, but the feeling of expectation. Of hope."

"Did you lose all hope when I entered the world?" Audrey said. "Or just when I slept with a guy I barely knew and got pregnant."

The technician laughed nervously. Lola rolled her eyes.

"Don't mind her. She just likes to make people anxious," Lola told the technician, giving her a feigned smile.

"It's going to be part of my top skills as a journalist," Audrey affirmed. "All my questions will be answered because they'll be too nervous not to answer them."

The technician finished up her scan and jotted down several notes. As Lola sat, watching, she was overwhelmed with the memory of the days when she had done this very thing. She had been the same age, with the same looks and a bit of the same spitfire sense of humor, although she thought Audrey was maybe a bit more sarcastic than she had been. She hadn't had many people in the city yet, and she'd dragged a brand new girlfriend along with her to the clinic. They had gone to a fast-food restaurant afterward and drank milkshakes. Lola had mostly cried into hers and wondered what the hell she was going to do, how she was going to support the baby. Although she felt pretty sure the friend hadn't had a clue how she would do it, either, she'd said all the right things. Lola had gotten through it in one piece as had Audrey.

After Audrey's appointment finished, they wandered out into the bright sunshine. The clinic was on the eastern edge of Oak Bluffs, near the long stretch of Joseph Sylvia State Beach. There was a little restaurant situated near the water, in full view of the glowing white sands and gorgeous blue waves. Audrey's stomach grumbled on cue. "I think we're both hungry," she said, grinning wildly.

Audrey and Lola were seated on one of the tables with white tablecloths, which were situated out on a dock overlooking the blue ocean. They ordered waters and fresh-squeezed lemonade. Lola watched Audrey scan the menu, her upper teeth caught over her lower lip. This had been the way she had always studied things with intense concentration, ever since she had been a little girl. It was funny that this tick had remained, although Lola would have never told her. She knew she had to treat Audrey with complete adult respect now. It would be a struggle, but she had to do it.

Lola ordered a salad, while Audrey ordered both a salad and a grilled cheese sandwich. They passed the menus back to the waiter and then blinked at each other in silence for a moment. It was almost a war. Who would decide what to say first?

Ultimately, it was Audrey.

"You never talk about my dad," she finally said.

Lola's lips parted. After a strange pause, she said, "Is that the only reason you showed me, Max? Because you wanted to know more about your father?"

Audrey shrugged. "A kind of courtesy, I guess. I give you my truth; you give me yours. Well, in this case, it's ours. I'm fifty percent of him."

"Only in DNA. I would say you're mostly me in all other ways," Lola affirmed, leaning back in her chair. She'd always known this day would come and it was one topic she knew she couldn't get out of.

The salads finally arrived. Lola grimaced and slotted her fork through a few shreds of spinach and, without looking at her daughter, said, "What do you want to know?"

"How did you meet him?" Audrey asked. "What did you like to do together? Why didn't he stay? That kind of stuff."

"Full range, I guess," Lola returned.

"You're a storyteller. I'm a storyteller. I guess it makes sense that I would want to know it all," Audrey said.

"Well, I can tell you that he was very nearly as handsome as your Max," Lola began. "So, I get the appeal of that. Hmm. What else? He was a writer. He loved to read. His book collection was extensive, but he just kind of stacked them all in the corner of the bedroom in this apartment he shared with five other guys. Oh! He was in a band."

"What did he play?" Audrey asked as she reached for the salt shaker.

"He played the bass," Lola said contemplatively. She remembered the way Timothy always furrowed his brow, in utter concentration as he played.

Now that she thought about it, he actually used to bite his lip just the way Audrey did now.

"How much do you remember about him?" Lola asked. "He left when you were four."

"Barely anything," Audrey said with a sigh. "I remember that he smoked cigarettes. He always stood on the back porch to smoke. I hated the smell. But I liked watching him in the darkness." She ended it with a shrug, as though what she'd said was no addition to the conversation at all.

But Lola could see the very image Audrey spoke of.

She could see Audrey there, four years old, a teddy bear pressed against her chest. She could see her watching her father outside, hoping and praying that he would return inside to pay attention to her, to play with her. When Timothy had left, Lola had demanded of him what she should tell Audrey when she got older. "How can I possibly explain to her that you left? How can I tell her that your only daughter wasn't enough to keep you here?"

Timothy had only cast his eyes to the ground. He hadn't been able to look at her. He had finally shrugged and walked off. He had taken his bass and left most of his books. A number of them still remained at Lola's residence in Boston. They still smelled vaguely of cigarettes. He had always said that he liked to smoke and read at the same time.

"Were you sad you had to raise me without him?" Audrey said, suddenly not breaking eye contact with her mother.

This felt like a very loaded question. Lola knew that it was about so much more than just herself and Timothy. It was about Max, too.

"No," she returned as she pushed her food around on her plate with her fork. "When he left, I realized how little he fit in with us. I knew that it would just be the two of us for a long time. And I was all right with that."

"But you must think about having someone longer term, now," Audrey returned. "Especially now that Christine and Susan are with Zach and Scott."

Again, Lola's mind trickled toward Tommy Gasbarro, that mysterious sailor. Her heart pumped with intrigue.

"To be honest with you, if love happens, it will be a blessing. If it doesn't, I still have enough blessings to last me the rest of my life," Lola returned with a smile. "You're the greatest gift of my life. Now, I have my sisters back; I'm getting to know my father again; I love my writing and I'm going to be a grandmother."

"What about Colin?" Audrey interjected. Speaking again of the editor, whom Lola had dated briefly ten years before.

"What are you talking about?"

"The way he looks at you," Audrey began with a shrug. "I'm sure if you asked him to move to Martha's Vineyard, he would consider it. I think he's loved you for years."

Lola marveled at her daughter's ability to see the inner workings of her life. She was so dumbstruck that Audrey giggled.

"Then I guess I'm correct," she said.

"Don't be such a smarty pants. It's not a good look," Lola said, rolling her eyes.

Audrey's grilled cheese arrived. The moment the sandwich was placed between them, Lola's stomach grumbled. Audrey formed a funny grin.

"I have a hunch one of us is regretting her salad decision?"

"Only one of us is eating for two, missy," Lola said. "Don't tempt me with all that cheese. It'll go straight to my thighs."

"Mmmm," Audrey said, digging into her gooey sandwich.

Lola scrunched her nose. After a long, dramatic pause, she quickly reached over, grabbed one of the halves, and took a big, cheesy bite.

"Hey!" Audrey cried as she playfully slapped her mother's hand away.

"Come on. I gave birth to you. I'm still collecting tax," Lola said, her mouth filled with brie.

CHAPTER 5

WHEN AUDREY AND LOLA RETURNED HOME, LOLA CHECKED her email to find that she had been called back to Boston by her editor, Colin, to discuss future projects, catch up, and celebrate the success of that Round-the-Island Race article. As Lola read the email, she couldn't help but think that Audrey could see the future. Colin very clearly wanted to check in for more reasons than business.

Still, Lola always missed Boston. It had been the place she had first made her home after those last strained and strange years with her father on Martha's Vineyard after her sisters had left her there alone. During those last years, Christine had only called a few times, and Susan had been altogether too busy with her wife and mother duties to bother. Lola didn't hold it against her any longer. It had been painful for all.

The following morning, Lola said goodbye to everyone, dotting a kiss on her father's cheek, making sure Audrey ate at least one nutritional thing for breakfast, and stopping by the bistro to grab a croissant from Christine. That busboy, Ronnie, manned the little window out front and grinned broadly at Lola as she approached.

"All of you look so similar," he said. "It's crazy."

"Actually, I'm Christine. We swapped places," Lola returned.

"I wouldn't be surprised. What can I get you?"

"Is that Lola?" Christine jumped up toward the window and beamed out. She had that frantic look to her eyes, which she always had when she had woken up before the crack of dawn. "Are you off to Boston?"

"Yep," Lola said, as Ronnie passed her a croissant in a little brown baggy. "It gets weirder and weirder to leave this place the longer we stay. I guess it kind of rubs off on you that way?"

Christine chuckled. "I don't even know the next time I'll have time to get off this rock. Enjoy it for me out there. Get some news from the outside world."

"Will do."

Again, Lola was mesmerized at Christine's chipper nature. Just before Lola turned back to walk toward the ferry, she caught sight of Zach through the window. He had hustled up behind Christine and wrapped her with his arms. She giggled and turned into him. Lola's heart surged with happiness for her older sister. If she was being honest with herself, she also felt a little hint of jealousy.

Maybe Audrey was right. Maybe she really was ready for some kind of love like that.

Still, she hadn't heard anything from Tommy Gasbarro. After her history of one night stands, very quick relationships, and brief flirtations, Lola had to guess that this was just another wisp of a fling. It had to be that way, regardless of how much she had thought maybe she had wanted it. Plus, there was the issue of his being Stan Ellis's ex-stepson.

On the ferry back to the mainland, Lola took notes for her upcoming story about a local artist on Martha's Vineyard, a woman she had gone to high school with who now commissioned multi-thousand dollar pieces for various celebrities on the island. Colin had been excited about the prospect of it, and she hoped to talk to him about it more when she arrived in Boston. There was nothing she liked more than unraveling a story with an editor, especially Colin since they got along so well.

Several hours later, Lola arrived in Boston via the car she kept in storage in Falmouth. As she entered the city, her heart surged with a mix of excitement and fear. She could still feel that old version of herself, the woman she had been at eighteen—fresh off the island and ready to conquer the world, or at least go after it. Timothy had put a dagger in it all and a baby in her belly, but that hadn't gotten in her way for good.

Whoever the hell this Max was, he wouldn't get in Audrey's way, either.

Lola parked the car outside of the office building, where she had worked for several years as one of the lead editors and journalists. Now, as a freelancer, she had a lot more freedom about what she wrote and definitely didn't miss the commute every day. As she entered, she thrust her shoulders back and felt her long tresses flow out behind her. She exuded confidence; she could feel it like heat coming off of her.

Colin Rainey stood near the printers on the far end of the main office building, speaking with one of the younger male journalists. When she entered, Colin turned his head quickly and immediately grinned in that mischievous way he always had. He broke off his conversation with the twenty-something immediately and strutted across the office. For a split second, Lola thought that maybe, just maybe, he was attractive. He was forty, with dark blonde hair and thick eyebrows and a perfect jawline. He kept good care of himself. Throughout all the years they had known one another, he'd only had two other girlfriends, besides the time he'd tried it out with Lola, of course.

Lola could feel it in everything he did as they walked toward his office. He loved her.

"Well, well. Look what the cat dragged in," Colin said.

"Ha. You mean, I'm suntanned, well-fed, and happier than ever?" Lola said, flipping her hair behind her shoulders.

"I guess I'm trying on sarcasm to hide my inner feelings of resentment," Colin replied, shutting the door closed behind him. "Martha's Vineyard! You always said you would never go back there."

Lola chuckled as she sat down. "I guess things change, huh?"

"But you never really explained why," Colin said. He furrowed his brow as he leaned against the edge of his desk, gazing into her eyes. "You just kind of up and asked to be freelance one day, and then, boom! Out of Boston altogether."

"I guess it's kind of difficult to explain," Lola offered as she sucked in a deep breath.

"Then let's grab some lunch, and you can tell me a bit more," Colin said.

Lola glanced at the clock. It was, in fact, just after twelve and she hadn't seen Colin in a good two months. She guessed she owed it to him to fess up and catch up.

Colin led Lola to their once-usual lunch spot down the street, a Mexican place with killer margaritas called Quando Quando. Normally, they saved the margarita drinking for after work, but Colin insisted they order a round with their lunch.

"Come on! I want to catch up. Really catch up," he told her.

Okay. Audrey had definitely been right.

"Well, I guess it's been a whirlwind," Lola tried. She took a tortilla chip from the pile in front of them and chewed at the edge delicately, feeling put on the spot. "My dad was diagnosed with dementia. My older sister, Susan, called us all back, and then, we learned about the secret of my mother's death. Apparently, it wasn't my dad in the boat all along. It was this guy she was having an affair with. A guy who's still on the island!"

Colin's eyes bugged out. "Holy crap. You've got to be kidding."

"I'm not. I'm a journalist. I'm sworn to facts," Lola said.

Colin burst into laughter, albeit a little too loudly. "I guess so. You were never that close with your sisters, right? I mean, since I've known you over the last ten years, I think you've brought them up maybe once or twice?"

"That's a bit complicated, too," Lola admitted. "We were close growing up until we all abandoned the Vineyard and tried to forget everything that had happened to us. Now, we're trying to repair our relationships."

"And how is that going?" Colin asked doubtfully.

"They're the best people I know on the planet," Lola said. She flared her nostrils, as though Colin's asking it had in some way insinuated that they couldn't have a second chance. "I wouldn't trade them for the world."

There was a strange pause. The server came to dot two

margaritas in front of them, frothy, with lines of salt around the edges. Colin always complained that Quando Quando put too much salt on the edges, while Lola had always loved the extra zap of flavor.

Colin lifted his margarita and said, "To new beginnings, then?"

"Absolutely. Thanks for saying that," Lola said, clinking her glass with his.

It seemed like Colin knew he had stepped in it and wanted to crank things back and re-generate the conversation. Since he was a journalist, he was able to do that almost seamlessly. The only trouble was that Lola was a journalist, too, and could see all the way through it.

By the time their food arrived, they had found a decent banter with one another.

"By the way, I really did enjoy your Round-the-Island article," Colin said, his mouth filled with cheesy quesadilla. Lola had always teased him for ordering that dish since she thought it was the equivalent of a child's order. Still, he stood by it.

"Thanks! It was really fun to write," Lola returned as she searched through her fajitas for a bit of sautéed green pepper.

"That guy seems like quite a character. Tommy..."

"Gasbarro," Lola finished.

"Right. We got a lot of emails about that article, actually," Colin continued. "A lot of our female readership was especially fascinated with him. One reader called him a hunk of a man. Her words, not mine." He leaned back in his chair as he dabbed his mouth with his napkin.

"Ha. I guess he is. He sails by himself almost constantly," Lola returned.

"But he crashed his boat, right?"

"It was an accident," Lola answered. When she blinked, she could still visualize Tommy in that hospital bed, the bandage wrapped around his skull. As she'd held his hand, she had thought endlessly about teenage Tommy meeting her mother for the first time all those years ago.

God. The idea of that nearly destroyed her. *Your mother was a remarkable woman. She made Stan laugh harder than I've ever seen him laugh before. Actually, I've never really seen him laugh since. I think the accident literally destroyed him. He would never tell me that, though. He's a hollowed-out person.*

"Lola? You still here?" Colin asked.

"Huh? Oh, sorry. What were you saying?"

"I just asked how Audrey is doing. She's at Penn State, right? She had that internship in Chicago?"

Lola grimaced and set down her fork. "Well, things went a little off the rails for Audrey."

"What happened?" Colin furrowed his brow. After all, he had known Audrey for many years and genuinely cared for her well-being.

"She got pregnant, actually," Lola said. "And she's going to have it, in case you were wondering that also."

Colin's lips formed a round O. "My gosh. That must have been a shock to the system."

"Sure. But it's not like I can blame her," Lola said with a sigh. "I had her when I was nineteen. I would never ever change anything. Not a moment of it."

"Time just kind of keeps going and hitting us with all these truth bombs, huh?" Colin said chuckling.

"Yes. I suppose so," Lola affirmed. She glanced at her empty margarita, paused, and said, "Do you want one more?"

Colin's grin was enormous, showing the slight gap between his two front teeth. A long time ago, Lola had thought that gap was terribly cute. Now, it was just a part of who he was—a man she had once liked, a man she now could only love as a friend.

At least, that's what she assumed?

There was so much to second guess in this life.

"Excuse me. Could we have two more margaritas?" Colin asked the server.

"Of course, sir," the server returned, collecting their emptied plates.

"Wonderful." As the server left, Colin leaned forward conspiratorially. "It's been such a weird year for you. Have you considered writing a book about it? I bet it would fly off the shelves."

Lola laughed good-naturedly. "You know, Colin, after I've had another margarita, I just might agree with you on that."

CHAPTER 6

LOLA STAYED IN FALMOUTH THAT EVENING AND RETURNED TO the Vineyard the following morning on the earliest ferry. Throughout the remainder of the afternoon with Colin, they had discussed the possible stories, edits to the brunch story, but never anything that couldn't have been done over email. It had both exasperated and excited Lola. She liked the idea of being wanted, regardless of who it was. She always had.

When she reached the Vineyard, Audrey waited for her, sucking down a Slurpee and listening to music in her AirPods as she leaned back on the front of the car. A small bit of skin poked out at her belly, which she assured Lola was only Slurpee gut, not a baby bump. Lola laughed and said, "You look ridiculous. All the tourists are staring at you."

"I know! I'm trying to give them a show," Audrey returned, before tossing Lola the keys to the car and placing herself in the passenger seat, a non-verbal decision not to be the driver.

Lola laughed and cranked the engine. Audrey slurped up the rest of her Slurpee and asked, "So, how did it go with your long lost lover, Colin?"

Lola blushed. "He's not my lover. We've been friends for years."

"Should I rephrase? How did it go with the guy who wants to get in your pant—"

"Audrey!" Lola called, swatting her on the shoulder playfully.

"What? I'm only speaking the truth," Audrey returned.

"I'll blame it on the pregnancy hormones this time. But not another peep about Colin out of you," Lola said, giggling.

"Someone spent the whole day flirting!"

"God. You're impossible."

When they reached the main house, they found Susan and Wes out on the back porch. Lola remembered with a jolt that Susan had another chemotherapy session that day, which she had promised to take her to. Susan gave her a sleepy smile and said, "How was the big city, little sis?"

Lola toyed with her glossy red curls and said, "Same as ever. Frantic and alive."

"Give me the beach any day," Susan said.

"You about ready to go?" Lola asked.

"Ready as I'll ever be," Susan affirmed. She rose slowly, pressing her hands against her lower back. "I'm just a frail old lady these days. Well, that's how I feel."

Lola opened her lips to say something, maybe a joke to match. Unfortunately, nothing came to mind. How could she possibly kid around about Susan's declining health? Instead, she wore an awkward smile across her cheeks and blinked at both Susan and her father and said, "Want me to bring anything from the store on the way back?"

"Hot dog buns," Wes said contemplatively. "I want to grill hot dogs. I think we're out of mustard, too."

"You've got it," Lola said, grateful to find some kind of meaning in the silliest of foods.

"Great call, Grandpa," Audrey said, slipping onto the porch swing next to him. "Me and this baby are craving hot dogs."

"And a salad," Lola said, pointing her finger. "And multivitamins! Remember that."

"Fig Newtons," Audrey said with a wink. "The most nutritional of all the cookies."

Lola grumbled, feigning exasperation. "I don't know what to do with any of you."

Lola drove Susan toward the hospital, grateful to have a bit of time alone with her. Susan adjusted her wig in the mirror and chatted about a new brand of mascara she had recently tried out. The conversation was painfully normal, the sort of thing they might have even talked about as teenagers if Susan hadn't left when Lola had been only twelve.

Lola and Susan walked back to the little room they had grown accustomed to over the previous weeks. Lola swept her arms over her chest and blinked out the back window at the docks and various sailboats, while the technician hooked Susan up to her chemo treatments. Lola's stomach clenched with fear and sadness. As though to mock her, Susan seemed serene, totally calm.

They tried to carry on some small talk for a while, but Susan soon fell silent. Lola returned to the window and peered out, her thoughts racing a million miles a minute. This had always been her mode of operation. Calm was in no way her brand.

"Amanda called me again about wedding dress shopping," Susan offered suddenly, her voice meek and far away.

"Oh. She wants to do that in Newark, I'm guessing?"

"Yes. I think so," Susan affirmed. "After the chemotherapy is over. I don't want to mess around with appointments and all that. It'll be annoying to have to bring this wig along with me, but I guess I'll be stuck with it for a long time." She chuckled then and added, "I've thought many times what Richard might think of it. He tried exactly once to get into role-playing with me. I played along as best as I could, but I already suspected he was cheating on me and I think the whole thing just turned me off."

"Richard sounds like a snake," Lola returned.

Susan, all-out laughed, then. "I wish I would have had you and Christine around to tell me that during my marriage. Still, we had a very good business for a very long time. And we had some damn good kids, so I did get a few things out of it."

"I love how much Amanda comes to visit you," Lola admitted. "I'm stuck with Audrey, but I don't think she would be here if she wasn't pregnant."

"Or as she dramatically says all the time... *with child*," Susan returned, giggling even more. "You're right, though. She's a free spirit, like you. Amanda is bound by duty."

"And love. She loves you more than anyone in the world," Lola reminded her.

"And I'm going to make it through this. Mostly for her," Susan said, her voice low. "Scott and Jake and the grandbabies and my beautiful sisters, you're all up there, too. But Amanda is my girl."

The words were powerful, true. Lola reached over and squeezed Susan's hand, unsure of what to say. She then turned her eyes toward the horizon to see a sailboat she hadn't spotted before, one she recognized from the race.

"My gosh. Tommy Gasbarro just docked his boat out there," she whispered.

"No way!" Susan said.

"Yes. I can see him from here," Lola said.

"Just as handsome as ever, I guess?" Susan asked.

"You haven't even seen him before!"

"I read your article, dummy," Susan said. "And Christine told me how smitten you are with him."

"I'm not smitten," Lola insisted.

"Right. You just rushed to the hospital after his injury, that's all," Susan returned.

Lola swallowed the lump in her throat. After a pause, she said, "He knew Mom. I'm fascinated with everything he might know about her. He... he knew her when she was my age. Right before the accident."

"Did he tell you anything else about her?" Susan asked. She jerked her head a tiny bit, her eyes electric.

"Not really. He was a little delirious. And when I emailed him, he didn't write back. I guess I imagined whatever connection I thought we had," Lola said with a light shrug. "It wouldn't be the first time. I've fallen for subjects of stories before. This was just a tiny bit different."

"I should say so," Susan offered.

"I just have never felt such peace when talking to someone," Lola said suddenly. She compared it in her head to her day with

Colin, and her stomach clenched. It was obvious in every cell of her body, which of the two men she preferred.

She was fascinated with Tommy, sure, but there was something else about him. Something that made her heart ache with promise.

She wanted to know him in every single sense of the word.

"You should go out there and talk to him," Susan offered.

"Um, what? Now?"

"I don't know what's holding you back. You're just standing there in the window staring at him," Susan said. "What happened to the Lola I used to know? The one who took life by the reins and charged forward, regardless of the consequences?"

"Maybe she grew up a tiny bit?" she said as she continued to look out the window.

"Please. When I called you to come to the Vineyard, you were literally at a nightclub," Susan said, rolling her eyes.

"I like music. So what?"

"You like the sailor more. Go out there. Just say, hi. What could it hurt? Besides. I'm basically tied to this chair. I can't get away. You can find me after you're done. I promise you won't miss a thing."

CHAPTER 7

Lola stepped out of the little room and back into the white and glossy hallway. Her heart pumped in her throat, and her hands felt strangely sweaty—reminiscent of long lost middle school days when she had been a tiny bit nervous around boys. She hadn't felt that so much since then. To her, throughout her twenties and thirties, men had been expendable—useful for very little except a night out and then, if all went well, a night in. Her friends in Boston had been envious of her ability not to grow attached. She had felt like it was a superpower.

Lola burst out the side door of the clinic and briefly adjusted her trendy bohemian dress in the reflection of the window. She wore gorgeous heels, which made her long legs look even longer and thinner, and her makeup was dark and smoky, something she had tried out in the hotel room in Falmouth that morning, just as an experiment.

To put it frankly, she felt terribly ready to approach the likes of

Tommy Gasbarro.

She drew her shoulders back and swept toward the staircase that led from the clinic down toward the docks. As her heels clicked across the boards of the dock, she remembered watching a teenage girl back in high school march down a very similar wooden dock in heels. She had gotten one of the heels caught between two boards and then been cast into the ocean, head-first, in front of many students. They hadn't allowed her to forget the incident for weeks.

Armed with this fresh fear, she felt her confidence wane slightly. Still, she trucked forward, until she neared Tommy Gasbarro and his gorgeous sailboat. He turned his face upward as she approached. Although he was far too stoic, handsome and masculine for such a thing, she thought perhaps he allowed the sides of his mouth to tweak upwards, if only slightly.

"Hi," Lola said. The syllable sounded insanely awkward, nothing the former version of Lola Sheridan would have ever mustered toward an object of her desire.

Stupid. She felt terribly stupid.

"Hey there," he responded. "How have you been?"

Lola's heart quickened. "Really good. Fine. You?"

"About as vague as all that," Tommy said. This time, he really did smile.

"I see you still have a bandage," Lola said. "Does it hurt?"

"Naw. Just don't want it to get infected," Tommy responded. He placed his hand over the bandage and shrugged.

"I thought maybe you were gone for good," Lola said. "I hadn't heard from you after you left the hospital."

"I come and go. Always out on the water or in some random seaside town," Tommy returned.

"Must be nice to be so carefree," Lola said playfully.

"It's the only life I've really ever known," Tommy said.

"Doesn't that get lonely?" Lola asked.

"I don't really know. I haven't thought about it much," Tommy said.

"Have you ever read The Old Man and the Sea?" Lola asked, shading her eyes from the sun.

"Hemingway? Sure. I've read it," Tommy said. "Hopefully, I'm not old enough quite yet for you to make that comparison."

"Not yet. Maybe they'll write a book about you. The not so old man and the Nantucket Sound," Lola returned.

"Maybe you should write it. After all, you've already given me more publicity than I would have ever hoped for," Tommy said. "I had a few people recognize me after I got out of the hospital due to the article you wrote. A kid asked for my autograph. It was weird."

"Did you give it to him?"

"Sure," Tommy said. "It was just a bunch of scribbles. I never really understood the appeal of an autograph. So what? I held a pen to a piece of paper and wiggled for a second."

Lola laughed a little too long. She hadn't expected Tommy to be actually funny. "Actually, it's good you brought that up."

"The autograph?"

"No. The writing thing. I would love to know what your next race is. Apparently, your article did so well for the publication that they wouldn't mind if I wrote about you every day. A kind of sea diary thing," Lola explained. All the while, she felt her cheeks burn with apprehension. Was it possible that she had already gone too far? She didn't want to scare him away.

"Actually, I'm headed down to the Florida Keys, to then sail all the way back to Martha's Vineyard," he said.

Lola's heart swelled with envy. "That's incredible. All that time on the water. Do you ever get bored?"

"What? No. Every day is different from the day before. The sky, the water, the air... it all comes together to form something like a new poem with every hour, even. Sometimes, if the waves are calm, I like to read or jot things down that come to mind. Otherwise, the time just passes differently when you're out there. It's difficult to explain if you haven't had a long journey like that," he said.

It sounded terribly romantic to Lola, although she knew this exact description probably didn't suit Tommy so well.

"You really should let me write a story about that," Lola said hurriedly. "I think our readers would love to learn more about what it's like to take such a long trek. Maybe we could set up an interview before you go and after you return so that you can compare what you thought it would be like to what it actually was. Would you be up for something like that?"

Tommy arched his brow. In the strange silence that followed, Lola felt almost positive that he was going to reject the entire idea.

Suddenly, however, he said the most surprising thing to her.

"Why don't you come along? Write those sea diaries you were talking about? Don't think you can properly write an article like that without a bit of your own perspective."

Lola was cool enough under pressure not to give herself away. That said, the second he suggested it, her heart started to beat a million miles a minute.

"That sounds good to me. As long as I won't be getting in the way?" Lola asked.

"I have a feeling that you'll find your way around the boat pretty easily," Tommy returned.

"I've been out a few times before. I don't think it's exactly like riding a bike, but..."

"It'll come back to you like that," Tommy said. He gave her a warm, handsome smile. "I leave in about a week. I can text you more of the details?"

"Sounds perfect," Lola said, matching his smile. "I look forward to it. An adventure! It's been a while since I had one of those."

"I tend to have one every few weeks. It's just how I've set up my life," Tommy said with a wink. "Let's get you back on track."

Lola said goodbye and spun on her heels, walking that long-legged strut back toward the clinic. Again, she was careful not to take a tumble. God, how embarrassing would that be after such a cool and collected conversation with her newest and perhaps most interesting crush?

When Lola arrived back in the clinic, Susan had finished up her chemo. She sat with glazed eyes in a waiting room chair, her purse across her lap. Despite the fatigue that was washed on her face, her wig looked absolutely spectacular, and her fashion was on-point, as always. Leave it to Susan Sheridan to look so put together in every stage of life, even the most sorrowful.

Susan's eyes perked up just the slightest bit when Lola entered. "There she is. What happened? You were out there quite a while."

"Sorry about that, sis," Lola said. She helped Susan to her feet and slowly guided her toward the sidewalk, lined with sunshine, outside the building. Once Susan had strapped herself into the passenger seat of their car, Lola licked her lips and said, "I think I just agreed to do one of the craziest things in my whole entire life."

Susan chuckled softly. "Crazier than that time you snuck into Leonardo DiCaprio's rented mansion in the mid-90s?"

Lola's eyebrows popped up. "How did you hear about that?"

"Gossip gets around this island. You should know that" Susan said with a wink.

"Well, yes. Maybe even crazier than that," Lola said, her cheeks burning at the memory.

"Wow. Fess up, Lorraine. What have you cooked up for yourself this time?"

"I just told Tommy Gasbarro that I would sail with him from the Florida Keys all the way back to Martha's Vineyard," Lola returned. In the silence that followed, she cranked the engine.

"Woah. You're right," Susan said as she lowered the volume on the radio. "This is big. Even for you."

"What do you mean? Even for me?" Lola said, chuckling.

"That's a lot of days on a boat with another person," Susan said. "I could be wrong, but I don't think you've spent that much time with any man since Timothy?"

Lola's cheeks burned. She turned the wheel and thought back to all her previous flings over the years, the men she had generally chewed up and tossed out.

"I guess there were a few overnight stays, trips to New York City, that kind of thing. Sometimes, there were work trips that turned into romantic flings. But you're right. However long this is, it'll be longer than anything else I've really experienced with a man since, gosh, Audrey was four years old."

"Crazy how time flies, huh?" Susan said.

"It gets crazier every time we have to say it," Lola returned.

CHAPTER 8

By the time they reached the main house, Susan admitted she was a bit too tired to socialize. Scott helped her to one of the new bedrooms downstairs and tucked her in. When he clipped the door closed and revealed himself again, he dotted his forehead with a handkerchief and turned his puppy dog eyes toward Lola, Christine, and Wes, who all stood around a little bowl of chips and salsa in the kitchen.

It was obvious that it was getting to Scott.

Hell, it was getting to all of them.

"How did it go up there today?" Scott asked Lola.

Lola shrugged and crossed her arms. "The same as ever, I guess."

"Yeah." Scott shoved his handkerchief back in his pocket and collapsed in a heap next to the table. Felix bounced up and slipped alongside Scott's leg, meowing. Scott placed a sad hand across his back, lost in his own thoughts.

Wes sat across from Scott and crossed his hands beneath his chin. "I know this must be hard for you, Son," he said. "But you're one of the only things keeper her sane right now. Don't lose faith. She'll beat this."

"Thanks for saying that," Scott returned. "It's easy to think that I haven't done anything to help her at all. It feels so helpless to watch someone in so much pain all the time."

Christine and Lola exchanged glances. It was bizarre that Scott spoke these words to Wes, especially since the Sheridan sisters all watched their father fall into a different, yet similarly heartbreaking state.

"I can't even tell her the news I heard about Chuck today," Scott continued.

"Oh? I haven't heard anything about that in a while," Christine said.

"Apparently, they saw him driving over the Maine border, back into New Hampshire. They couldn't track him after that; seems like he cut off the main road and somehow lost them. But he's still in the country. I have a hunch that he's spending more money than he thought he would. I wonder where he hid the rest of it. It can't be tied up in any bank accounts that we know about," Scott said. He scrubbed his hands over his eyes again and heaved a sigh. "That said, it's not like I can focus on this at all. Susan and the Inn are my main focus right now."

"Of course," Lola murmured. "I don't think any of us expect you to catch your criminal brother at a time like this. I'm sure the authorities will catch him sooner than later. It only takes one wrong move."

"You're right," Wes affirmed. "It's not even a priority right now.

The Inn survived it. The other places he stole from also survived it. He's living high right now, sure, but he's lonelier than he's ever been. We still have the Vineyard. We still have each other."

Zach hollered a greeting from the door that led out toward the driveway. He entered, whipping his blonde hair as he strode into the house, and delivered a kiss to Christine's cheek. In his hand, he held a bottle of wine, and his grin was handsome, his skin sun-kissed and healthy.

Immediately, he sensed that he had entered something a little grimmer than he had anticipated. "I'm sorry. Am I interrupting something?" He arched an eyebrow as he looked around at everyone.

"Not at all," Wes said. "I was just fighting the girls over this bag of chips."

"Ha. Take it away from me," Christine said with a smile. Then playfully swatted her father's hand.

"It's a hot one today. I have the itch to go swimming," Zach said.

"Why don't we all go?" Christine said before she snapped her fingers, her eyes bugging out. "Or, what if we went waterskiing? We haven't gone since we were teenagers. Lola, you must miss it more than any of us. You were like the best on the island."

Lola's cheeks burned. "I wouldn't go that far."

"It's totally true," Christine affirmed, grinning from ear to ear.

"Actually, I remember that. You won a few of the summertime contests. You blew some of the best tourists out of the water," Zach said.

Everyone admitted that this was the perfect solution to keep their minds busy that afternoon. Quickly, they changed into their bathing suits and headed toward Scott's boat. Scott agreed to drive, although he admitted he'd never been one for waterskiing. "I will break every bone in my body if I go," he said.

Down in the boat, Lola snapped one of the straps of Christine's bright yellow and black polka dot one-piece. Christine yelped and spun around.

"Nice suit, Sis," Lola said with a grin.

"I like yours, too. Once I hit forty, I traded out the two-piece for a one," Christine said.

"You know you could still rock a bikini," Lola said.

Christine rolled her eyes and lifted the bag of chips from the side of the boat. "But where would I put these?"

Lola chuckled and tossed her head back. The sea breeze swept through her hair and tossed it in every direction, making her shriek with pleasure. That moment, Scott cranked the engine, as Zach began to assemble the waterski rope and waterski back up on the dock beside them.

"Who's going first?" he called over the sound of the motor.

Christine pressed her elbow into Lola's side.

"Me?" Lola cried. "I haven't gone in twenty years."

"Yeah? Well, I haven't gone in twenty-three years," Christine said. "I guess that makes you the expert here."

Feigning annoyance, Lola sauntered back out onto the dock, donned a lifejacket, and slipped both feet into a single waterski.

"You're going straight for one ski?" Christine called.

"Sure. I'm not a wimp," Lola returned as she flashed her sister a grin.

"You did just say that you haven't done this in twenty years. Make it easy on yourself, old woman!" Christine hollered.

The boat had begun to ripple away from the dock. This left Lola very little time. She gripped the plastic handle attached to the long rope and felt her legs quake. This wasn't like riding a bike; this was a lot more like having a huge motorized water vehicle drag you across the waves as you held yourself aloft on your hopefully still strong enough legs.

Lola dropped into the water and adjusted her weight. Her hands held onto that plastic handle for dear life. She nodded toward Christine, who told Scott to hit the gas. There was a roar, and Lola's heart surged. She was lifted up and out of the water and soon found herself riding forward, centered on that waterski—only adjusting her balance a few times. Immediately, the wind struck her cheeks and her forehead and flipped her hair out behind her beautifully. She felt strong, alive, and a huge smile flashed across her face. In the boat, Christine jumped up and down, clapping her hands.

This was the same thing Christine had done when she had helped Lola learn how to waterski way, way back in the day. Susan had been there, too, as had their mother. It had been a huge day for them—bringing the youngest sister along on one of the family's favorite activities. Anna, namely, had been incredibly good at the sport. Lola remembered how long and powerful her legs had looked when she had erupted from the waves. She had envied and adored her mother. She had wanted to be just like her.

Now, she kind of hoped that she wasn't so much like her.

She hoped she would never give up on her family the way Anna had.

The memory of this caused Lola to lose strength. When Scott whipped the boat back toward the dock, Christine rotated her finger through the air to ask if Lola wanted to go around again. Lola shook her head violently, no. She dropped the plastic handle and allowed herself to sink into the water near the dock again. Scott yanked the boat around and buzzed over to her, where she had already unlatched herself from the waterski.

"How did it feel?" Christine asked.

"It felt amazing," Lola said. "You have to go next."

Christine turned her eyes toward Zach. Lola sensed a brief moment's hesitation. Christine had always been the weaker of the three sisters when it came to waterskiing. Lola had always suspected this was due to her fear of the speed, of the water, and of embarrassment at falling in front of everyone else.

"You should go, baby," Zach coaxed, drawing a strand of hair behind her ear.

"Okay. Just don't laugh if I don't get up," Christine said.

Christine leaped into the water. When she erupted back into the air, she yelped and laughed like a little kid. She managed to slip into the lifejacket while treading water, then took the ski from Lola as Lola swam back toward the boat. When Lola climbed back up onto the motorboat, she flipped her hair back and waved down at her older sister. All the color had drained from her cheeks. She was clearly terrified.

"You got this!" Lola called out. Then she gave her sister a thumbs up.

"If you say so!"

Lola turned back to spot Scott, seated in the driver's seat, his face tanned and a slight smile across his face.

"How are you doing, Scott? The driving getting boring for you at all?" Lola asked.

"Naw. I love it," Scott said. "Any excuse to drive the boat around is fine by me."

Christine took a few tries before she fully yanked herself up. By the time she got it, she had looked a tiny bit exasperated, but totally thrilled. Lola clapped her hands wildly and punched the air in celebration. Christine mouthed something to Lola through the air. If Lola wasn't mistaken, it was something like, *Don't make fun of me.* Lola mouthed back; *I'm not!* She shoved her tongue out of her mouth, mocking her, and Christine burst into laughter and nearly fell from her ski.

After Christine, Zach took a turn and mesmerized them with his daredevil qualities. He whipped in and out of the wake, tossing himself around like an Olympic skier. His abs and muscled glistened in the sunlight. Christine wolf-whistled when he finished, then leaped into the waves to hug him tightly and kiss him. Their joy was infectious; their love was akin to the love of teenagers. Still, Scott and Lola pretended they were annoyed and rolled their eyes.

"Give it a rest, guys!" Scott called.

When they got back to the dock, they found Amanda and Audrey seated at the edge of it with their toes in the water and large glasses of lemonade in their hands.

"We saw you!" Amanda called.

"How did we look?" Lola asked. She leaped out of the boat and latched it to the side of the dock, making sure to double tie it, just like Wes had taught her some thirty years before.

"Like very, talented people," Audrey said. "You never told me that you could do that, Mom."

"Didn't I?" Lola said, surprised. "Maybe there are even more secrets about me; you don't know."

"Can you juggle?" Audrey asked.

"No."

"Can you speak Swedish?" Audrey asked.

"No."

"Then I'm not interested," Audrey said teasingly.

Everyone piled off the boat and sauntered back up toward the main house. Susan had gotten out of bed to watch the festivities from the porch swing, and Wes sat beside her, nursing a cup of tea.

"You guys look better than ever," Susan said.

"We just need our third Sheridan sister out there with us," Lola said. She grabbed a towel from the stack on the porch and wrapped it around her shoulders, shivering suddenly.

"The second I'm ready, I'll let you know," Susan returned. "I hadn't realized how much I missed it until I saw you whizz through the air. It's the freest feeling in the world."

"Free. And terrifying," Christine said.

Apparently, Audrey and Amanda had spent most of the day together, shopping in Edgartown and Oaks Bluff and hiking at Felix Neck. Amanda grabbed some of their shopping bags, and the girls brought out a few items they'd bought, including a little light pink onesie they had purchased for the baby that said, "Vineyard Girl," on it.

"Again, I don't think there's any way you know it's a girl," Zach said to Audrey, chuckling.

"You keep dismissing my women's intuition!" Audrey said.

"Regardless, if the baby is a girl or a boy, he or she will have an appreciation for Vineyard Girls, at least," Susan offered, ever mindful and able to seek a compromise. "He or she will wear the onesie with pride."

"He or she will probably wear the onesie without knowing that pink is a girl color and those words mean anything at all," Lola interjected.

"Uh, oh. Grandma has spoken," Audrey said, chuckling.

Again, Lola felt the idea of that like a jolt. A grandmother? How was that possible? She was only thirty-eight, the same age as her mother. The last age of her mother.

Meekly, she gave Audrey a smile.

"Uh, oh. It seems like you age shamed her!" Christine teased.

"Mom. You know you're a youth," Audrey said, rolling her eyes. "Like everyone at Penn State thought you were my sister."

"Let's change the subject," Susan said. Her voice had brightened considerably since her treatment earlier that day. "I think we had better start to think about dinner."

It was agreed that this was the only way forward. Lola, Christine, and Audrey banded together to make up some sloppy joes. Wes got on the phone with Aunt Kerry, and soon, both she and Uncle Trevor crowded around the picnic table with the rest of them and dug into their meal. Laughter rang out from the big house; conversation topics were far-reaching and charted everything from Lola's long ago waterski competitions to Christine's newest method for baking apple pie to Audrey's decision that Fig Newtons weren't so good for the baby, after all.

Mid-way through the meal, Susan announced to everyone that Lola was headed out for a dramatic writing assignment. Lola grimaced as all eyes turned toward her. She wasn't sure how to break this news to everyone—least of all, Christine.

"That sailor I featured for the Round-the-Island Race. I'm headed out with him next week. We're going to sail from Florida back up to Martha's Vineyard," Lola said, careful to keep her voice from wavering.

Christine's eyes narrowed. "Tommy Gasbarro?"

"Yes, Christine... that's his name. As you know," Lola said, finding the sarcasm again in her voice.

"I think that sounds marvelous," Aunt Kerry said. "It's been ages since I was out on a sailboat like that. Trevor, we really should try to take our boat out more often."

"Does that mean you'll miss your birthday?" Audrey interjected suddenly. She held her sloppy joe aloft, both hands gripping its sides.

"I guess so," Lola said. Her heart stirred with apprehension, but she kept her smile bright.

"Your thirty-ninth. Spent out at sea," Susan marveled at the idea.

The strangeness of the number—the one their mother hadn't made it to—hit everyone at once. Silence filled the table for a moment, before Christine finally said, "And you really think you can trust this guy?"

"Christine, come on," Susan said. She shot her sister a look.

"Susan, I don't mean to take over your position as the sensible one, but Tommy Gasbarro did crash his boat during the Round-the-Island Race. We watched it happen. I just don't want something like that to happen to Lola," Christine blurted.

Again, nobody seemed to know what to say. Audrey placed her sloppy joe back on her plate and licked the edge of her thumb contemplatively. Scott rose up and asked if anyone wanted a beer. Zach and Wes both admitted they did. Amanda chimed in next, with a, "Me too! If it's not too much trouble."

"I think you're going to do great," Susan said softly, speaking directly toward Lola. "If anything, I want to hear about another Lola adventure. I guess I missed out on your wilder years." Again, she clucked her tongue and added, "That gosh darn Leonardo DiCaprio party."

"Mom!" Audrey cried. "You didn't tell me about anything like that."

Lola's cheeks burned again. All this attention was usually a welcome thing for her; she supposed her embarrassment came from a genuine interest in Tommy Gasbarro, something she had to question, as he was Stan Ellis's ex-stepson.

"Come on. Tell us at least one thing about the Leonardo DiCaprio party," Amanda insisted, cracking open her beer. "I think you owe it to us now."

Lola gave a fake-grumble, then leaned forward conspiratorially. "Well, it all started because one of my best friends, Hannah, dared my other best friend, Monica, to kiss someone at least partially famous that summer. Since the Vineyard is constantly streaming with celebrities, it seemed like an okay bet that something like that could happen. We were seventeen, I think, and Monica had just lost a little bit of weight and gotten a new wardrobe and, yada yada yada, she was feeling herself."

"Yada yada yada," Christine chimed in, grinning wider.

"We heard about the Leonardo DiCaprio party from a friend who worked in catering for some of the high-end catering companies," Lola continued. "And he said he thought he could sneak us in if we wore all white over our fancy party clothes, like we worked with him, then change after we got in. So that's exactly what we did."

"Mom!" Audrey said, her eyes wide. "You wild child."

"You have no idea." Christine shook her head, all-out abandoning the rest of her sloppy joe to focus wholly on her sister's tale.

"There were loads of celebrities from the nineties there," Lola continued. "Including Jonathan Taylor Thomas, who was extra special at the time and, around our age. When Monica saw him, she grabbed Hannah's arm and said, 'That's the one! I'm going to do it. I'm going to talk to him.' But I did a really bad thing." Lola's cheeks burned even brighter as her family leaned in. "I beat her to it."

"You didn't!" Susan cried.

Lola burst into laughter. "To be honest, the kiss wasn't even that good. I had much better with some people here in Oak Bluffs. But you should have seen Monica's face when she caught us. I thought she was going to eat me alive."

"Are you saying my dad could have been Jonathan Taylor Thomas?" Audrey cried. "Man. Imagine our lives, Mom. We could be living in Los Angeles, bumming around with celebrities."

"And instead, boo-hoo, we live on Martha's Vineyard," Lola said, rolling her eyes. "What a tough life."

"But what about Leo?" Amanda asked, nearly swooning. "Did you see him anywhere?"

"He was up on the balcony talking to Claire Danes for a while," Lola admitted. "She was the prettiest thing about that party, except for the chocolate fountain, which me and the girls obviously hit hard on the way out. I can't remember when I snuck back in the house. It must have been after three or four."

Wes shook his head. "I had zero chance when it came to you."

He laughed. "I never knew what you were going to do next, and I never really knew when you were coming home. But you always cooked me dinner. No matter how frantic your social life was, how busy you were with school, or what duties I made you perform at the Inn, you always had something either on the stove, in the fridge, or in the freezer. I'll never forget that."

Lola had actually forgotten that. Although she loved the memory of kissing Jonathan Taylor Thomas beneath the enormous August moon, she loved more that she'd been the kind of daughter her father could count on. What they'd lacked in communication, she had tried to make up for in whatever way she could. Probably, on some level, she had wanted so much more from him and he from her. But they'd done what they could to get by, while the other sisters made lives elsewhere.

CHAPTER 9

THE NIGHT BEFORE LOLA'S DEPARTURE WITH TOMMY Gasbarro across the wild American countryside, down the Atlantic coast and toward the southern tip of Florida, Monica and Hannah suggested they get together for a few drinks in downtown Oak Bluffs "for old times' sake." Lola hadn't been able to catch up with them in a few weeks, due to family and work obligations, but the story of Jonathan Taylor Thomas and that long-lost raucous party at the mansion outside of Edgartown had put a fire in her belly to hold her two dearest and oldest friends close.

Monica was a beautiful and curvy blonde, with two teenage boys and a burly contractor husband, whom she had met during college at Penn State. Lola pulled up to Monica's place first and spotted the two teenage boys out back, kicking a soccer ball lazily back and forth while drinking sodas. Their names were Tyler and Kevin, and they were spitting images of their six-foot-four father— the kind of soon to be men who you always asked to help you move.

Monica appeared in the doorway and yelped. "Lola! You're here!" She ran out of the house in a little leopard print number that surged over her breasts. She wrapped Lola in a big hug. "Oh, honey, how has it been? How is your sister? Can I get you a drink while we wait for Hannah?"

Lola sat with Monica on the front porch and watched the world go by with a first glass of wine. She told Monica that she had informed her family about the Jonathan Taylor Thomas incident, and Monica burst into gut-wrenching laughter and said, "You didn't! Tell me you didn't ruin my reputation like that. I can't have everyone know you stole Jonathan Taylor Thomas away from me."

"To be honest, I think he's had a pretty good life without either of us," Lola said, chuckling.

"His loss," Monica said.

As Monica explained a little bit more about the frustrations of being a mother to two teenage boys (monstrously messy, it sounded like), Hannah pulled up in her truck and hopped out. She had gone grey a tiny bit early and allowed it to happen, the lighter strands mixing with her darker ones in a way that looked artistic and interesting, rather than "sad" and "old." Hannah herself worked in jewelry making and owned a little shop in Edgartown. On the side, she read tourists' tarot cards, which she reported brought in the most money of all.

"People love knowing their future," she had explained. "We're all so anxious about it. I like to give them at least a tiny bit of peace of mind."

Hannah had a younger child, a girl, age eleven. Unlike Lola and Monica, she'd taken her time before she'd had a kid, traveling a bit across both Europe and Asia. She had learned to make jewelry in Thailand and had decided to bring the skill back. Hannah had always been a little out there in a way that made Lola surprised that she remained on the island after so many years. She had always anticipated Hannah living in a hut on the beach of Bali or hiking through the mountains of Poland.

Still, she was grateful to have her there with them.

Hannah, Monica, and Lola walked toward a craft beer place in Oak Bluffs called Offshore Ale Co. Lola ordered an IPA while Hannah grabbed a wheat beer and Monica went for the red ale. Together, they sat at a table overlooking the street.

"I'm heading out tomorrow," Lola said, scrunching her nose. "I'm a little bit terrified, to be honest."

"Our Lola? Afraid of something?" Hannah said scoffing. "No way. I don't believe it."

"I'm afraid it's true," Lola said, heaving a sigh. "This guy— Tommy Gasbarro. He's different. When we look at each other, it's like sparks go off between us."

Hannah and Monica made eye contact. It seemed like they could communicate without words. Lola remembered when she'd had this with them, as well. She had lost it a bit since she had been away the longest.

"What's up?" Lola demanded.

"Nothing," Monica said hurriedly.

"Well. It's just." Hannah gave a light shrug. "You talk about him so differently than you've ever talked about anyone."

"You hardly even liked that guy you had a baby with," Monica pointed out, shifting forward a bit so that her breasts bulged out even more from her leopard print. "When you called me about him you were like, Timothy messed up again. Timothy won't shower. Timothy, Timothy, Timothy..."

"He was really good at that bass, though," Lola said with a smile.

"Girl! Anyone can play the bass," Hanna returned. "You know that."

"I can't blame Timothy for everything. I wanted to have the baby. He wanted to keep reading Nietzsche and not doing the dishes. I think it all worked out fine," Lola said.

Their conversation turned to other things. Hannah talked about her daughter's new interest in making jewelry; Monica talked about Tyler and Kevin's new interest in eating every single item in the fridge and still being hungry after.

After their first two beers, Monica suggested they head over to Jaws Bridge to watch an August sunset and swim in the Nantucket Sound. Lola, now accustomed again to Vineyard summers, had her swimsuit packed. Spontaneous swims were a part of the game.

They stopped briefly at Monica's to change into their suits and pick up a bottle of wine and some plastic cups, then walked the thin beachline toward Jaw's Bridge, where part of the '70s horror flick had been filmed. Together, they splashed into the water, crying out at the streaks of orange and pink above the glittering blue. Lola floated for a while as the waves shifted against her, tilting her back toward the shore. Her heart thudded loudly in her ears.

All she could think about was what might happen next.

Surely, she and Tommy would have to stay at a hotel on the way to Florida.

What would happen there?

Would they share a bed?

Would he kiss her?

And what about on the boat, out there on the open water?

There was sexual tension between them. That was clear.

But did she actually want to get involved with him? After all, he was a loner and seemed to want that life and only that life, forevermore.

Back on the sand, Monica popped open the bottle of wine and poured them each stiff glasses.

"I forgot that when Monica's our bartender, things get sloshy really fast," Lola said, snickering.

"The pours have gotten a lot bigger since the boys became teenagers. I can assure you of that," Monica said.

"But are they really as bad as we were?" Hannah asked. "We were always getting into so much trouble. Lola, your dad, didn't really care what you did, it seemed like, but my mom nearly killed me when she caught us going through her liquor cabinet. Oh, and all those parties. Remember when we saw Ben Affleck and Gwyneth Paltrow together?"

"A very different time," Lola admitted. "I always remind people they were together and they have to look it up. They don't believe me."

"We had a really unique childhood," Monica said with a sigh. "I guess our children do, too."

"And Audrey's getting into that now," Lola said. "She's fallen totally in love with the island. And with my family. It's enough to make me really guilty that I kept it away from her for so long."

"Does she want you to date again?" Hannah asked. "My daughter is a little apprehensive about it. She's still young, but her dad only left two years ago. I wouldn't be surprised if it takes her a little bit longer."

"That makes sense. I probably would have flipped if Dad was dating when I was a teenager," Lola replied. "That said, Audrey really wants me to date. She has a hunch that my editor in Boston has a huge crush on me."

Monica smirked. "Of course he does. You're Lola Sheridan."

"Come on. Whatever," she retorted, rolling her eyes.

"Seriously, though. What does this guy think of you running off with this sailor? I'm assuming he's the editor working on the story with you?"

"He approved it, yeah," Lola said. "He basically told me I could write about whatever I want."

"Wow," Hannah said. "Have you considered him as an option at all?"

"Audrey suspects that he would move to the island for me if I wanted him to," Lola said. "I just don't know if it's ever been really right between us, you know? We tried about ten years ago, and it just wasn't a perfect fit. Which makes me think that you're pickier when you're twenty-eight than when you're thirty-eight? Gosh, I mean, I'm almost thirty-nine. Maybe I should just give in already."

"Where's the fun in that?" Monica asked.

The women returned to the water several more times, watching as the stars twinkled in from beyond and the last wisps of sunset dulled out. When they finished the bottle of wine, they walked back to Monica's house and sat out on her porch, chatting amicably with Tyler and Kevin about calculus and soccer practice and next year's prom, waiting for Audrey to come pick Lola up to bring her home. When Audrey arrived, she ambled up to the house and placed her hands on her hips.

"Haven't the tables turned?" she said, grinning wildly. "Let's get you home, Lola Sheridan."

"You're the spitting image of your old mom," Hannah said, dotting a kiss on Audrey's cheek. "Good to see you again, Aud."

"You too, Hannah. I have to get this lady back home so she can rest up for her big adventure tomorrow. She thinks she can drink all night and drive all the next day? She's not nineteen anymore," Audrey said teasingly.

"You'd be surprised what I can do," Lola said. She tossed her arm over her daughter's shoulder and waved to her friends with her other. "I'll see you girls when I get back from the open seas. I'll be thirty-nine by then, you know. Thirty-nine years old, with my whole life ahead of me. Er—half of it, anyway."

Back in the car, Audrey rolled her eyes at her mom and said, "I guess my baby will be just as embarrassed by me in nineteen years, huh?"

"It's a part of the equation," Lola said, dropping her head on the car seat headrest and gazing at the stars again. "It's the circle of life."

CHAPTER 10

LOLA SOBERED UP QUICKLY THAT NIGHT AND FOUND IT RATHER difficult to sleep. This turned into a kind of panic of circular thoughts. *If I can't get to sleep now, then I won't be well-rested for the trip, and I won't be able to help Tommy drive. Then, Tommy will think I'm useless and will regret having invited me. I need to sleep. Come on, Lorraine! Sleep!*

Of course, that kind of thinking was of no use at all.

Around eleven-thirty in the evening, she shot up from her bed and headed toward the hallway. Downstairs, she heard the soft sounds of Audrey and Amanda's voices in the bedroom they shared —probably passing secrets and gossip. She rubbed her eyes and turned her head spontaneously to the right. To her surprise, the ladder hung down from the attic.

Lola stepped toward the ladder and gripped one of the lower rungs. She peered into the darkness. At the far edge of the little hole, there was a soft glow, proof that someone was still up there, snooping around.

Lola didn't want to call out, as she knew that would wake her father. Instead, she took several delicate steps up the ladder and then entered the dark haze of the attic. Susan, without her wig, wearing the lilac robe that had once belonged to their mother, sat cross-legged in front of the chest where they had originally found their mother's letters and the diaries. The sound of Lola's footfalls forced Susan's face around quickly. At first, she looked panicked, as though Lola were a ghost.

"Don't worry. I'm not her," Lola said, her voice low.

Susan exhaled slowly. "I know. I just got so lost in my own thoughts up here. I wanted to go through this old trunk to find some extra stuff to decorate the new bedrooms with. There are loads of beautiful photographs in here of the three of us. Some full family photos also."

Lola perched next to Susan to analyze what she had found. In several of the photos, Susan held Lola in her arms and smiled at the camera. Susan was a full six years older than Lola and had long-operated as her stand-in mother, especially when Anna and Wes had had too many responsibilities at the Inn.

"I remember when you wore this dress," Susan whispered, waving around a photo in which Lola wore a red-checkered number, one that would have been better suited on a doll. "I loved it so much that I had one similar made for Amanda when she was born. It was like déjà vu, holding her so many years after I had dressed you in it."

"Nice you got all that practice being a mother before you did it for yourself," Lola said. "When I first had Audrey, it sometimes took me three tries to get the diaper right."

"Ha. Precision was never your specialty, either," Susan said.

"Gee. Thanks." Lola stuck out her tongue playfully.

"Don't take it too hard."

They continued through the photos and old paperwork and awards, including Susan's "Top Ten Student" graduation diploma, one of Lola's waterskiing competition trophies, and a sad poem Christine had written once, which, apparently, their mother had framed.

"Should we show Christine this?" Lola asked.

"I'm not sure. It's a tiny bit emo, don't you think?"

"Maybe. It's so far away from how she is now," Lola said.

"She looks like she's always about to float away with happiness. Like Peter Pan," Susan said.

Susan continued to flick through the photos, even long after Lola grew bored. Just before Lola thought she'd better return to her bed to attempt some level of sleep, Susan clucked her tongue and said, "Who is this?"

"Let me see," Lola said.

Susan passed a photo of their mother, probably mid-to-late-thirties, standing next to a teenage boy of sixteen or seventeen years old. The boy was handsome, with jet black hair and broad shoulders. His smile was confident, as though he'd just told a spectacular joke. Lola lifted it more toward the light; her lips parted in shock.

"You're never going to believe this," she said. "But, I'm pretty sure that's Tommy Gasbarro."

"No way," Susan breathed.

Lola flipped the photo over for some kind of description. Sure enough, in the top right corner, their mother had written the letters: T+A, 1992. The year before her death.

"Wow," Lola breathed. "How strange is it to find this here now?"

"I guess Stan must have taken the photo?" Susan said. "It looks like they're over in Edgartown. Huh. I can't believe she was so close with Stan that she actually became so close with Tommy, too."

"Do you mind if I take this with me?" Lola said.

"On the trip? With the guy in the photo?" Susan asked, arching her brow. Her tone very much asked, *Whatever you're planning on doing, is it actually a good idea?*

"Sure. I'm guessing he'll want it, anyway. I don't think we plan to put it up in the house anywhere," Lola said.

"Okay. You're right. Just make sure you don't make too many messes on that trip of yours," Susan said. She rubbed at her upper forehead, where her hairline had once been. "I know that's your style, but remember that there will be some of us back here, worrying about you endlessly."

"I know. I'll be careful," Lola said.

Lola and Susan gathered up the photos and trinkets Susan had decided on for the rooms downstairs. Lola slowly stepped down the ladder and then acted as a spot beneath Susan as she descended. Obviously, she was weaker than she had been when they'd first crawled up there. Lola wanted to scold her about even heading up there alone, but she knew she would face the wrath of the ever-individualistic Susan Sheridan and she wasn't a glutton for punishment.

Back in her bedroom, Lola placed the photo of Tommy and

Anna on her bedside table and then slept fitfully for another few hours. Her eyes popped open again with their own agenda around four in the morning. Annoyed, she hobbled out of bed and wandered downstairs, where she found Christine brewing up a first pot of coffee, making lists, and preparing for the day ahead.

"Good morning, sunshine!" she said. "I didn't expect you up this early."

"Wow. You're chipper at four in the morning," Lola said, pouring herself a first cup of coffee. "I didn't expect that."

"Every day, I become more and more of an optimist," Christine said as she snapped the end of her pen.

"Disgusting," Lola said sarcastically. "I can hardly look at you. You're as bright as the sun."

Lola showered and dressed quickly, then grabbed her already-packed bag and headed to the bistro with Christine. Once there, Christine snapped on the lights and draped an apron around her waist, tying it behind. She then tossed an apron to Lola, who didn't catch it in time.

"Sorry. I guess my reflexes don't kick-in until five-thirty," Lola said.

Christine chuckled and turned on the radio. "We're going to make some croissants, some banana bread, and a few pies this morning. My new intern is starting today, as well, so I'm looking forward to showing her the ropes. She just moved to the island to take care of her ailing mother."

"Sounds familiar," Lola said. "Did she go to school with us?"

"She's maybe thirty-five," Christine said. "So we missed her by a bit. She went to culinary and pastry chef school late, also.

Actually, when I asked her about her twenties, she was a little bit cagey."

"Maybe she committed a crime. Or just has a dark past," Lola offered.

"I'm sure you'll have plenty of time to ask her when she gets here. You'll be kneading bread until you have to leave. When is that exactly?"

"I'm meeting Tommy at the ferry at eight," Lola confirmed.

"Fantastic. I'll get some good, hard labor out of you yet," Christine said.

Christine showed Lola a few basic techniques for early-step croissant formation. Lola was surprised at how soul-affirming the work was. It was much different than writing an article or a short story. Whatever muscle you put into it, so to speak, would eventually surface as a gorgeous croissant or piece of banana bread or a slice of pie. Every action had a direct result. An article, on the other hand, had maybe an emotional reaction out there in the world —but it was much harder to quantify.

About thirty minutes into their work, Christine's new intern, Winona, arrived. She was a red-headed spitfire of a girl with bright blue eyes and an infectious smile. She shook Christine and Lola's hand, to which Lola said, "Oh, don't worry. You don't have to impress me at all today. Just her. She's the boss."

Winona laughed. "I remember you, Lola. You were a senior when I was a freshman in high school. We used to run on the track team together."

Lola tried to fumble through the images she had of the girls on the freshman track team. "Oh, maybe I remember you."

"It's okay. You don't have to pretend," Winona said. "It's not like I remember any of the freshmen who were around when I was about to graduate. I was ready to get off the Vineyard!"

"Us, too," Christine said. "And look at us all here again. Back where we belong?"

Winona chuckled. "As long as you can teach me everything, you know. I think I've read about every article that's been written about you, Christine. It's a damn shame I never made it to Chez Frank. It was on my radar the minute it opened."

"Ah! Were you living in New York at the time?" Christine asked.

"I was in and out. I spent a bit of time in Sweden because I met this guy in a band and moved there with him for a while. Every time I made any decision the past fifteen-odd years, my mom has kind of just shrugged and said, 'Whatever. It's your life.' But now that she's sick, I figured it was time for me to suck it up and put in the time here. I don't mind at all. Actually, after being so many places, I think Martha's Vineyard is prettier than ever."

"We feel the same way. About pretty much everything you said," Lola said with a wide smile.

As they kneaded the bread, Lola spoke lightly about the adventure she was about to go out on—noting how casual she spoke about it with this other assuredly brave and confident woman. She was, after all, the sort of woman who just moved to Sweden at the drop of a hat.

"And you're going to sail all the way up from Florida?" Winona breathed. "Oh my gosh. I can't wait to read the account of this."

Zach burst in through the ever-flapping kitchen door and grinned at them. His teeth seemed whiter and fresher than ever, as though they reflected the sun above.

"Christine, I see you've captured some helpers for your prosperous bakery window!"

"I took them hostage, yes," Christine said. She lifted her chin and dotted a kiss on Zach's lips. "You ready for the big rush today? The governor of Vermont will be here."

"I remember, darling," Zach said. "Everything is prepped and ready to go. Ronnie has been told to practice his meditation before the shift starts."

"Meditation?" Winona asked.

"Ronnie is our favorite busboy, but he's prone to panic," Christine said. "He's fainted twice during rushes. Zach has to go out and scrape him up off the floor and dust him off."

"He's lucky I haven't had to use a spatula yet," Zach said with a wink.

Lola finished up at the bistro at seven-forty-five, which gave her enough time to pour herself a to-go cup of coffee and kiss Christine goodbye. Christine, whose face was covered in flour, beamed at Lola and whispered, "Do us proud out there on the open seas. And force him to talk about mom. We'll be here when you get back."

"As a thirty-nine-year-old," Lola marveled.

"Yep. A thirty-nine-year-old," Christine returned sadly. "All grown up."

CHAPTER 11

Lola arrived at the ferry dock just before eight. She held a little brown baggy filled with two croissants, and her eyes scanned the fifty-some tourists, hunting for some sign of that handsome bachelor. According to Tommy, he had already loaded up his boat on a rental trailer on the mainland, which they would then attach to a rental vehicle to drive all the way down south. Still, it felt odd to find Tommy Gasbarro, sailor extraordinaire, seated on one of the ferry boat benches, his eyes cast toward the horizon line, deep in thought.

"You boarded without me," Lola said.

Tommy started slightly, then grinned. "Sorry about that. I figured there was really only one place to check where I was."

"I guess so." Lola passed him a croissant, which he held in his large hands and blinked down at it. "This looks beautiful. Better than anything I've seen in Europe."

"Really? My sister, Christine, made them. Have you sailed a lot in Europe?"

"Yes," he answered. "I spent a lot of time in the French Riviera, hence the croissant knowledge, and nearly a year around the Greek Islands. Perfect water over there."

"I call BS. Nothing more perfect than our Vineyard water," Lola returned with a cheeky grin.

The ferry boat cranked off the dock. Tommy bit into the edge of the croissant and muttered, "Flaky crust. Gooey insides. My god. Is she a magician?"

"Maybe," Lola said. "I've grown up thinking both of my older sisters are fascinating. We're all so different, although we do love to tease each other to high heaven."

"It's a good pastime," Tommy agreed. "Can't take anything too seriously."

"We try not to," Lola said.

They fell into easy banter after that. Lola talked briefly about her recent trip to Boston. Tommy asked her if she missed her life there. Her answer, "Sometimes yes, sometimes no," seemed to make more sense to him than it might have to other people. After all, he was so transient.

"I miss every place I've ever been," he offered. "And I know I'll already miss the sailboat after we get off of it and return here."

"It's exhausting, spending your life missing things all the time," Lola said.

"That's why I just try to always have something to look forward to," Tommy said.

"A good way to live."

"The only way, I think," Tommy affirmed. "By the way, has the interview already begun for the article?"

"Good question," Lola said, chuckling. "I have a whole list of questions, but I think I'll probably begin the proper article when we get down to Florida."

"So this is all off the record?" he asked her.

"Yeah. So if you have any murders you want to confess, you can do that now," Lola said, flashing a smile.

Tommy burst into another of his infectious laughter fits. Lola's stomach flip-flopped with excitement.

She was on a trip with a man.

It would be just her and Tommy, like this, for the next week or so.

It was enough to make her head spin with joy.

When they reached the mainland, Tommy led Lola toward the parking lot, where he'd had a valet prepare the rental and the boat trailer behind it. He placed a twenty in the valet's hand and thanked him, then ducked around to open the passenger side for Lola.

"A sailor and a gentleman? Is that even scientifically possible?" Lola asked as she slipped inside.

"I'm sure it'll come back to bite me one day," Tommy said. He hustled back around and strapped himself in, then added, "Stan is the one who instilled a lot of that stuff in me, by the way. The door opening. The manners. He doesn't seem like that kind of guy now, but he sure as heck was back in the day."

Lola pressed her lips closed, unsure of what to say. Tommy cranked the engine and pointed the car's nose in the direction of the main highway, out of Falmouth and away from the region of the world, she knew the most.

After the first shock of hearing Stan's name again wore off, Lola found her way to other topics of conversation.

"Have you sailed in Florida before as well?"

"Oh, yeah. The Keys are fantastic," he told her. He drove in an attractive way with one hand on the top of the wheel and the other just hanging down below, occasionally tapping in time to the beat from the radio.

"So basically, your rule over the years has been, if there's water, you're headed there to sail on it?" Lola asked.

"I guess so. I pictured myself as a kind of modern-day explorer. Sure, you can look up photos of those places and dream up what they might be like. But I want to witness them myself. I want to feel that sand between my toes. I want to know the people and the cuisine."

"And you're always, always a stranger," Lola affirmed.

"I guess so," Tommy said. "But it's something I like. Nobody knows me, but they reveal what they want to me, and I reveal what I want to them. It's like everything in my life is a first impression. I never dig down deeper than that, because you don't really have to. First impressions are always correct."

"Do you think so?" Lola asked.

Tommy chuckled. "I thought you said that the interview portion wasn't until later?"

"I'm just curious. What did you think of me when I first met you out on the dock?"

"I already knew who you were. Your reputation preceded you," Tommy answered.

Lola's heart pounded. "You knew my mother, and you knew of us girls. But that's it."

"The youngest Sheridan girl? The wild one? I've heard stories," Tommy said, his eyes glittering. "I spent more time on the island in the years after your mother— And I spotted you around. People said you always snuck into celebrity parties. They said you got on yachts with governors. They said that your father couldn't keep up with you, so he had stopped trying long ago."

"Did you believe them?"

"They're good stories, even if they're not true," Tommy returned. "So, I guess I would like to believe them."

Lola blushed. "They're true," she said meekly. "But I had to teach myself how to grow up pretty soon after I left the island. All my fun and games stopped for a while since I had a daughter at the young age of nineteen after I got to Boston."

"Huh. That's a punch in the face, isn't it?"

"It's definitely a way to end the party fast," Lola agreed.

The drive to Key Largo, Florida, would take them approximately twenty-four hours in total. On this first day, headed slightly west and slightly south, they planned to drive a full twelve hours and stop about half-way, in Fayetteville, North Carolina.

"I've never been to North Carolina," Lola said.

"I spent a whole summer in Asheville once in my twenties," Tommy said.

"How could you possibly? It's nowhere near the water," Lola said, ogling the map displayed on her phone.

"Mountains are certainly a close second in terms of natural beauty for me," Tommy said. "I scoured those Smoky Mountains. I guess it didn't hurt that I had met a girl there and she wanted me to stay."

"Wow. The loner Tommy Gasbarro, settling down with a girl," Lola said.

"Like I said. I only made it the one summer," Tommy said, flashing his eyes toward Lola conspiratorially. "She was a fantastic woman, but she wanted much more than I could give her."

Lola swallowed the lump in her throat. Had he said that because he wanted her to know that they could never be anything?

Again, she reminded herself that this whole affair was strictly business.

She was there to write a story. To get up close and personal, in the style of more traditional journalists who followed the story wherever it went.

Out her window, Lola spotted Providence, which they very nearly touched before cutting south and west down the coast. Just a bit later, she spotted the New York skyline. Her heart leaped with excitement.

"I always thought I would make it to New York," she said, adjusting the radio station to a more local channel as it phased out. "One of those frantic New York reporters, you know? Covering some of the biggest stories in the world."

"I never liked New York," Tommy said.

"That's the biggest surprise in the world," Lola said, giving him a sarcastic smile.

Tommy shrugged. "It's not that I don't get what people like about it. All those cultures coming together. All that food! As a half-Italian man, I can definitely get behind Little Italy."

"Maybe you could join the mafia?" Lola said, chuckling.

"I don't think they would have me," Tommy said. "I don't work so well with others."

They cut out from New York and then eased into New Jersey, which was beautiful, despite its reputation. "I never understood why people looked down on this place so much," Lola said.

Between New York and Philadelphia, Tommy yanked the car over at a rest area with a few attached restaurants. It was just afternoon, and he admitted he had already burned all the way through Christine's croissant and needed sustenance. He parked next to the gas tank, got out, and began to fill the rental. It struck Lola as strange, watching this man perform this very normal action. In some ways, she saw herself as everyone else in the parking lot did: as his girlfriend or wife, waiting for him to fill up their car so they could eat together and talk about normal things, like health insurance or a baseball game.

It surprised her now how much that kind of "normal" life thrilled her.

Inside, Tommy and Lola grabbed sandwiches and quickly ate them in the little dining area, where a toddler smashed a plastic spoon against his mother's thigh again and again. Tommy told Lola they didn't have much time to waste since he wanted to make Fayetteville before nine-thirty if possible. On the way out, Lola grabbed a few snacks and drinks to sustain them. When Tommy arched his brow at them, she shrugged and said, "Haven't you ever been on a road trip before?"

"Of course I've been on a road trip before," Tommy said back at the car, ripping open a bag of Twizzlers and popping one between his lips. "But not with another person in a long time, frankly. It's not as fun to eat yourself silly when you're by yourself."

"Oh! That reminds me. You should let me drive," Lola said, grateful that her fatigue from barely sleeping the night before hadn't caught up with her. "Seriously. It would be my pleasure. Unless you're too much of a control freak?"

Tommy chuckled and rapped his palms against the top of the car. "I am, of course, a control freak. But I would like to lean back for a bit. My shoulders get so stiff when I drive for long periods of time."

"Then it's settled." Lola grabbed the keys and slipped into the driver's seat. She shivered with excitement, feeling Tommy's eyes on her as she tapped the gas and thrust them out of the parking lot. About fifteen minutes into the journey, she asked, "How am I doing so far?"

"Should I give you a grade?" Tommy asked.

"Maybe just a pass or fail."

"Okay, then. You pass," Tommy said with a mischievous grin.

"I better not be close to failing in your book," Lola said. "I'm going just a little over the speed limit. I'm between the lines. I passed that slow car a bit ago. I think I'm doing fantastic."

"I wish we could use all that confidence as fuel for the car," Tommy said. "We would get all the way to Key Largo.

When they reached Fayetteville that night, it was nine-fifteen— fifteen minutes before Tommy's set time goal. Lola's heart thudded with excitement. It had been a glorious day, one of the most beautiful in recent memory. She felt she could have sat and talked with Tommy Gasbarro for many more hours.

At the hotel front desk, Tommy asked for separate bedrooms. Lola felt the words like a punch in the stomach; after all, she was much more accustomed to guys who pushed their luck, who tried to go a little too far. Did this mean that Tommy wasn't attracted to her? Tommy turned to give her the key to her room and then said, "I'm so beat. Mind if I turn in? We have another long day tomorrow."

Lola's voice felt far away. "Of course. I'm tired, too. Should we meet at the continental breakfast at seven?"

"Perfect," Tommy said. "Sleep well, Lola. Don't let the bed bugs bite."

"If you brought us to a hotel with bed bugs, I swear I'll..."

Tommy walked away, laughing mid-way through her sentence. Lola held her bag by the front desk, watching him go. She felt the concierge's eyes on her, as though he wanted some kind of explanation for why Tommy had asked for two rooms.

Shut up, Lola. It's not like everyone is so obsessed with your story. Nobody will even remember you were here tomorrow. That's how hotels work.

CHAPTER 12

THE NEXT DAY IN THE CAR, AUDREY WOULDN'T GIVE THE
texts a rest.

AUDREY: Come on. Have you kissed him yet?

AUDREY: Just give us SOME kind of update, jeesh.

AUDREY: Christine says she's going nuts and just needs to
know when the wedding is, so she can plan out the cake.

AUDREY: MOM!

But Lola refused to give her any answer except:

LOLA: I'm having a good time and looking forward to writing
the story. He's a fascinating human being. Thanks for asking!

At this, Audrey sent her an exasperated-emoji and stopped her
rampant texting, at least for the time being.

They drove through the rest of North Carolina, dipped into
South Carolina, then entered Georgia close to Savannah, a place
Lola had always wanted to visit due to its incredible history of art.
As they skidded through the rest of Georgia, Lola's stomach

clenched with excitement. When they hit Florida, she felt she could hardly stand it.

Tommy told her he had planned for the sailing trek to take between four and five days. "I've never known a woman so up for not having a proper shower for that long," he told her.

"I've never met a man so game for hanging around a smelly lady for that long," Lola returned with a smile.

"How do you plan to write as we go along?" Tommy asked. "Notebook? Computer?"

"I have both with me," Lola admitted. "But any time you need my help, I'll put everything away."

"I trust you," he said. "I don't know why. But I do."

When they reached Key Largo, it was eight-forty-five. The sun had already set, but the beaches swelled with tourists, with partiers, and music. They parked the rental in a lot near a beach-side restaurant and padded across the sand. Lola's fingers fluttered against Tommy's, but she quickly pulled her hand away.

"I'm starving," Tommy admitted, as the host sat them at a table near the water. He gazed out across the waves as the moonlight illuminated his handsome face.

"Me too," Lola said, remembering a few moments too late that she hadn't answered yet.

The server came to take their order. Lola ordered swordfish, Tommy salmon. They decided to share some garlic bread to start. Lola also ordered a glass of white wine, which pushed Tommy to add a beer. This was the sort of thing people on dates did; they indulged and drank. They spoke about their lives.

Still, Lola felt it too difficult to press Tommy for more details about Stan Ellis, about her mother. That photograph Susan had found upstairs remained in between pages of her notebook. She had no idea when she would feel ready to bring it out.

After eating heartily, Lola and Tommy checked in to a nearby hotel and agreed to meet the following morning around eight-thirty to return the car to the rental company and prep the boat. On the drive, they had made a list of groceries and other supplies, which Lola said she would purchase while Tommy finished with the boat. She would show the receipt to Tommy later, and he would reimburse her for half.

At the store the following morning, she loaded her cart with fruits, cereal, nuts and seeds, beef jerky, fixings for sandwiches, a few sweet treats, and even a few bottles of wine, just in case the air and water became calm and they wanted to relax and watch the sunset. *Have deep, soul-searching conversations. Fall in love*—that kind of thing.

Shut up, Lola, she said to herself.

At check-out, the woman behind her seemed like she was preparing for the same kind of trip.

"Which way are you sailing?" the woman asked her.

"Up to Martha's Vineyard," Lola affirmed.

"Wow! Four days? Five?"

"Something like that," Lola said. "He's the sailor. I'm just along for the ride."

"You're going to love every minute of it," the woman said. "The first time my husband took me on-board, I thought I was going to throw up, I was so nervous. Now, we try to take major trips like that four or five times a year. It'll change your life."

Lola grinned, conscious that she had totally left out the fact that Tommy wasn't anything to her but a story idea. She loved living in this fiction.

Tommy stood as a confident and powerful sailor at the edge of the boat, watching as Lola approached with several bags of groceries. He beamed at her, then cut down from the boat to help her on.

"How did it go?" he asked.

"Good, I think. I got everything on the list, including sunscreen. You forgot to add sunscreen," she told him.

"Ah! That is such a necessity. You're right," he told her. "We would have fried."

Tommy was a professional. You could feel it in everything he did on-board, the way he handled the sails and whipped them out of the harbor. Lola turned quickly to watch the gorgeous white sands of Key Largo fade into the distance. Droplets from the Atlantic shot past her cheeks. The sun, the air, the wind, it was all different than the far south—foreign, almost nothing like the summer sun at Martha's Vineyard.

"Wahoo!" Tommy cried.

For the first hour, Lola felt as young and alive as a teenage girl. She stood at the edge of the boat in bare feet, gripping one of the rods and gazing into the impossible blue below. She felt Tommy's eyes on her, watching her legs, her movements. He kept the sails broad, taut, and he played music from a little speaker that he'd tied to one of the rods on the opposite side. They surged across the Atlantic, making good time. Around them, Lola could see no other boats. There was no way to prove that any other human on the planet existed besides her and Tommy.

"Have you seen many sharks?" Lola asked, perching at the edge of the boat and grabbing a bag of trail mix.

"Of course," Tommy affirmed. "They are such large, powerful creatures. Those large hungry black eyes..."

"I guess that's a funny last thought as they eat you," Lola said. "What a hungry beast!"

"Ha. Be careful with all that teasing. If we encounter any sharks, and it's between you or me, you know I'll feed you to them," Tommy's voice trailed over her.

"Just let me send off the article first, so that I can be remembered," Lola said.

Lola decided that it was high time she sat down with her notebook to jot down some ideas for the article, especially since she was so mesmerized with the first few hours of the process. Plus, she wanted to remember the drive, Key Largo, all of it—if not for the article, for herself.

I've never seen a man so comfortable with a boat. The sailboat seems almost like an extension of Tommy Gasbarro's body, as though he was born with more than just skeleton and muscle. He sweeps across this beast of a sailboat, whistling, seeming to know and understand every single crash in the wave and tilt of the wind.

For this reason, I find it even more incredible that he crashed his boat during the Round-the-Island Race. When he brought it up more recently, he said, "I can't believe I misjudged that gust of wind. It hasn't happened to me like that in a really long time. A rookie mistake if I've ever seen one." You can tell the shame will live with him for a long time.

I sailed a long time ago with my father, mother, Susan, and Christine. I must have been eight or nine, which means, Christine was around eleven or twelve and Susan was fourteen or fifteen. Mom and Dad, of course, got into some kind of fight on-board, with Mom declaring that Dad wasn't a fit sailor. I didn't know, at the time, that Mom was looking for any reason to belittle Dad.

Tommy plopped down beside Lola and tried to steal a glance at her journal, but Lola placed a hand over her writing and said, "Hey! Mind your own business."

"Are you writing all about me? I'm doing my best to perform for you," Tommy said, his grin growing wider.

"Not everything is about you."

"This article is."

"Fair enough," Lola said. She nodded toward the western horizon, where a sunset had begun to brew. "Looks like we're going to have a beautiful one tonight."

"That's the thing about being out in open water," Tommy said. "No matter where you are, you get a good sunset. It doesn't matter if you're on the east coast or the west."

Lola snuck into her bag to grab a bottle of wine.

"What do you have there?" Tommy asked.

"I think we have reason to celebrate, don't you?"

Lola found two glasses of wine in the kitchenette and poured them hefty portions. When Tommy had his in-hand, they clinked glasses and, for a moment, gazed into one another's eyes. After they sipped, there was a strange silence, the kind Lola might have filled with a kiss if it had been any other guy.

"Have you ever slept on a boat overnight before?" Tommy asked her.

Lola shook her head. "No. This will be my first time."

"You'll never sleep better in all your life. It's like being in a cradle as a baby. That is unless the waves get too frantic."

"I guess that would make it a little more like a rickety carnival ride," Lola said, trying to envision her own analogy.

"Something like that, yeah," Tommy said.

Lola prepared them sandwiches for a pre-sleep treat. Both admitted they were exhausted. After eating, Lola excused herself to the private area on the other side of the boat to change into an old t-shirt and a pair of shorts to sleep in. She washed her face and then collapsed in one of the two beds, which were located next to the kitchenette, beneath an overhang. Just before she drifted off, her phone got a smidge of data and an email came through from Colin.

Hey! No idea if you can receive this out there on the open seas. I just wanted to check in and wish you luck. I know the article is going to be great. See you when you're back on land.

Lola turned to look at Tommy, who remained out in the darkness. He had removed his shirt, and the moonlight enhanced his washboard abs. He gazed out across the waters. Despite her otherwise unmatched creativity, Lola could hardly imagine what his thoughts might be. He was sometimes a total mystery to her. She was coming to really love that about him.

CHAPTER 13

THE THIRD DAY OUT TO SEA WAS LOLA'S THIRTY-NINTH
birthday. Her eyes popped open right at sun-up when the sky was a
delicious cotton candy and the heat wasn't yet set to scorch. She
slipped out from beneath her blanket and let herself look for just a
moment at the still-sleeping Tommy in the bed on the other side of
the little enclosed arena. His wild black curls spilled out across the
pillow, and one of his large hands stretched across his chest. Lola
wondered if a man who lived such a carefree life in the world ever
bothered to dream. He had already lived so many of her greatest
fantasies. He had seen it all.

Outside, Lola slipped into her swimsuit and then stretched out
to greet the sun. She felt apprehensive, and she wanted to shake it.
She performed a few yoga routines out on the front of the boat,
hoping that an easy stretch might clear her head. Still, with every
shift of her limbs and every creak of her bones, she was reminded of
the gravity of this day.

Lola Sheridan was now thirty-nine years old.

Older than her mother had ever been.

When Tommy woke up, he wandered into the sunlight without a shirt. Inside the kitchenette, the coffee maker had begun to pop and bubble.

"You're up early," he said, beaming at her.

Again, her heart jumped. She wondered if she should tell him about her birthday. Then again, it seemed to add strange pressure to the situation. What would he say, anyway? Congratulations? It didn't matter. Time existed differently out on the water.

Still, she felt morose in ways she hadn't anticipated, especially as she helped Tommy with the early-morning preparations on the boat. He informed her that they were making good time, that they would probably make it to the Vineyard at the end of the fourth day, tomorrow. Lola instantly felt a pang of regret.

"It's going to be hard to get off of this boat," she said truthfully. "I can see why you're so addicted."

"It's nice, pretending the real world doesn't exist," Tommy agreed.

Just after mid-day, Lola sat to write in her notebook, while Tommy read a book across from her, occasionally getting up to adjust the sails. He had talked several times about the sheer exhaustion of operating a sailboat alone—that he had hardly gotten more than two or three hours of sleep per night and felt continually hungry and thirsty, but he had said it like he was an explorer and this was just part of the business of discovering a new world.

When Lola turned the page of her notebook, she was surprised to find Tommy and Anna Sheridan's photo. She blinked down at the gorgeous photo of her young mother, aged thirty-seven, and she placed her hand over her heart. This was the woman who had given birth to her thirty-nine years ago. She hadn't heard her voice since she was eleven-years-old.

"What's wrong, Lola?" Tommy said suddenly.

Lola's eyelashes fluttered up.

"You look like you've just seen a ghost."

Slowly, Lola lifted the photo from the notebook and passed it toward him. Tommy gripped the edge with two firm fingers and gasped.

"I've never seen this photo before," he said. "But I remember this day really clearly."

Lola's heart swelled with sadness, with fear. Where had the Sheridan sisters been when that photo had been taken? Why hadn't Anna spent every moment of her dwindling life with them?

Why had she been with Tommy, the ex-stepson of her lover?

"She was so kind to me," Tommy continued, still gazing at the photo. "I was sixteen here, I guess? Something like that. She talked to me for hours on this day, in particular about getting into college. She made me promise her that I would take the SAT. You know, I actually did take it the next year, early '93. Didn't do so bad either. We celebrated the next time I came to the Vineyard. That might have been the last time I ever saw her."

Lola's stomach flipped. She couldn't muster anything to say back.

"I didn't make it to college, though," he said. "I knew Anna would have been disappointed."

Tommy tried to return the photo, but Lola didn't reach for it. "You should keep it," she said. "It's your memory. Not mine."

Tommy furrowed his brow. He seemed just to have realized

there was something a bit off about Lola. Lola wished she could yank herself out of whatever dark shadow had just passed over her.

What was it about birthdays that made them swallow you whole?

Anna had never spoken to Lola about college. Anna hadn't been around for Lola's SAT. Lola had taken the SAT during a post-party hangover. Wes had forgotten to pick Lola up from the SAT, which she had taken in Edgartown, and she'd met up with Monica and Hannah afterward and started drinking in the afternoon on the beach.

Anna hadn't been around because of Stan, the person who had brought Tommy into Lola's life, in a sense; the person that had turned off the lights on his boat, a misstep that had cost Anna Sheridan her life.

Stan Ellis had ruined everything.

Suddenly, Tommy bucked his head toward the eastern horizon and said, "Oh no. Look." He slipped the photo into his wallet and then shot toward the sails.

Black and grey and purple clouds billowed in the distance. Lola shivered. The wind shifted and became strange, yanking the sail in several different directions at once. From the look on Tommy's face, it was obvious that things were about to get turbulent.

"Lola? I need you to stop sitting on your ass and start helping me," Tommy said.

Lola balked. "Excuse me?" Nobody spoke to her like that. Ever. Especially not on her birthday. Who did he think he was?

Tommy grimaced. "We're going to capsize if you don't help me. Do you understand?"

Lola popped into action, following Tommy's lead to bring up

the storm sails, which were much smaller but proportioned for higher winds. The waves thrust toward the boat, and Tommy steered them directly into them, screaming to Lola, "Hang on tight!"

Lola didn't have to be told twice. She was absolutely petrified. The clouds above were now monstrously dark, thicker than she had ever seen, and the water beneath them had a mind of its own, as though a huge creature lurked beneath them and prepared to bubble to the surface. Lightning rocketed out of the sky and connected with the water, and large, fat raindrops barreled down upon them. All the while, Tommy operated the boat with a cool and concentrated demeanor.

Still, the storm seemed to go on forever. Lola was completely drenched and shivering, still in just a swimsuit stationed on one side of the boat, clinging to a rod for dear life. Every few thoughts involved her mother. Why had her mother allowed them to ride in the dark like that, without lights? Why had the beautiful and whip-smart Anna Sheridan abandoned her family in the night and allow herself to be injured so badly that she'd drowned?

Now, history was on the verge of repeating itself.

Here, on the thirty-ninth birthday of Anna Sheridan look-alike Lola Sheridan's life, she was inches from being tossed off-board and into the frantic Atlantic waves below.

The only person she had to rely on was Stan Ellis's ex-stepson.

What the hell had she been thinking?

What would Audrey do without her?

Tommy lurched to the side of the boat and adjusted the sails again. His eyes scanned toward Lola, but his face was volatile and stoic, with nothing of the flirtation they'd once had.

"Did you really think sailing directly into a storm would do us any good?" Lola cried to him suddenly, fully realizing the depths of her anger and fear.

"Yeah. Like I did this on purpose?" Tommy blared.

"Aren't you supposed to be keeping tabs on the weather?" Lola demanded.

Tommy rolled his eyes and turned back, clearly annoyed. Lola didn't have time to dwell on his feelings. She kept her eyes on the clouds and willed them, with every beat of her heart, to calm down.

It took maybe another thirty minutes for the storm to subside. When the waves slowed, Lola glanced at her hands. The knuckles were white as bone since she had clung to the rods so hard. Tommy busied himself, changing out the sails with rugged yet sure tugs on various ropes. He did not look at Lola. He seemed enraged.

Suddenly, Lola's knees gave out from under her. She fell onto the floor and curled up and suddenly burst into tears. She placed her forehead on her knees as her entire body shook. It was only in safety that she realized the depths of her fears. It was only in the haze of the afterthought that she perceived the fact that she might have died, really and truly died, like her mother before her.

When she lifted her head again, she found Tommy seated across from her. He studied her, his face difficult to read. One thing was clear. He hadn't sat down to attempt to console her. His eyes were hard.

"Lola, we're out of the storm. Everything is fine now," he told her.

He sounded like her dad, trying to reason with her when she had been upset during the years after Christine and Susan had left her behind.

"I—I know." Lola refused to apologize for it. "I just. I couldn't stop thinking about my mother. About Stan."

Tommy's eyes looked increasingly stormy, as though they'd captured a tiny bit of the sky before it had moved south.

"You have to trust that I know what I'm doing," Tommy affirmed. "I've done countless trips like this. I've waged war on many, many storms."

And yet, the first time I saw you sail, you crashed and ended up in the hospital.

Lola knew better than to include this particular thought in the conversation. She didn't answer. Her tears dried to salt on her cheeks.

Tommy reached into his pocket and drew back out the photo she had given him before the storm. He flapped it around in the now-still air. "Tell me, Lola. Why are you really here with me on this trip?"

Lola flared her nostrils. "I'm pretty sure you were the one that invited me."

"Yes, I did. But why are you really here? Actually? Are you here because you want to dwell in the past? Are you here because you want me to fulfill some kind of empty feeling you have surrounding your mother?"

"Actually, Tommy, all I've done the past twenty years is try to run away from the past," Lola blurted. "The fact that I'm even facing you—a representation of that past—is pretty remarkable."

"But that just means I'm a tool for you. Something to make you feel like you've grown as a person," Tommy returned.

"That's not true," Lola said. She sputtered, rage replacing all her fear. "In fact, regardless of what I feel or felt about this whole journey, it's obvious that you're such a loner that you would never face what might exist here—between us. You just want to keep living whatever shadow of a life you've had the past twenty-five years. You don't want to be anyone for anyone, so you'll just keep running."

Tommy sniffed. "Is that how you feel?"

Lola sputtered. "I don't know, Tommy. I just know I can't look at you right now."

"So much for facing your past," Tommy blared.

"God. Why won't you shut up," Lola muttered as she sauntered back into the sleeping area. She fell across the mattress and burrowed her face in her pillow. Devastation flowed through her. She couldn't believe how stupid she had been. She'd actually built up some romantic ideas around Tommy Gasbarro. She had actually thought going on this trip would be the soul-search she'd needed to enter her thirty-ninth year.

Instead, she had just been reminded that she could never escape the past, that her own mortality was always much closer than she thought, and that Tommy Gasbarro was no future. Not for her and not for anyone else. He would make sure of that.

CHAPTER 14

LOLA AND TOMMY KEPT THEIR DISTANCE FROM ONE ANOTHER
for the remainder of the trip, as best as they could, at least, given the
fact that they were two people trapped together on a sailboat in the
middle of the Atlantic Ocean. Lola busied herself with the article,
writing little notes to herself about what she had perceived were
the bigger struggles of a solo sailor, along with the fact that Tommy
had hardly slept for several days in a row. Although she made a
point of not speaking to Tommy, she still prepared meals for him,
conscious that he'd upped his manpower in order to direct the
sailboat back toward the Vineyard.

Lola wanted to mention the shift in the air to Tommy, the fact
that what had been Florida air had gradually eased to their familiar,
gorgeous late-summer New England air—an air that seemed looser
and freer, with a touch of nostalgia to it. This nostalgia, Lola knew,
was all connected to the fact that September was right around the
corner. With September came the end of the tourist season, the end

of summer, and with that, the island cleared off until next spring, allowing the residents to breathe a collective sigh of relief, reorganize, and prepare for the off-season ahead. Although Lola hadn't seen an off-season in twenty years, she remembered the sadness and the relief that it normally brought.

When the Vineyard first came into view, Lola's heart leaped. It was a grey and green rock billowing up on the horizon line, a bit blurry due to the clouds and the surf. Tommy instructed her with sterile words so that she could assist him as they docked. Lola obeyed, asking questions when she needed to, but making sure not to make any eye contact.

As the boat drew closer, Lola spotted a tiny crowd around the dock. With a lurch, she realized that Christine, Zach, and Audrey stood out on the edge of it, holding up a sign that said, "HAPPY BIRTHDAY, LOLA!" Tommy turned his head toward her and grunted.

Finally, he asked, "When was your birthday?"

"Yesterday."

Right. The worst-possible day ever. The day they had bickered and ended whatever had been brewing between them—that day.

They docked the boat. Audrey hollered, "That's right, Mom! Look at you! A real sailor!"

"Ha. Don't make fun of me," Lola said, hopping off the boat and swallowing her daughter in a massive hug.

"I can't believe you actually made it," Christine cried, giving her another hug. "Four full days out to sea! That's insane."

"Did she drive you nuts, Tommy?" Zach asked.

Tommy remained on the boat. He strung his fingers through his black hair and seemed at a loss for words. "We had a good trip," he said finally. "Only one storm. A monster of a storm, but it's in the past now."

"Sounds like you have some war stories." Christine beamed.

"Let me help you get your stuff out of here," Zach said. "We took one of the bigger vehicles from the Inn and—surprise—we have something planned back at the house."

"Not another classic Sheridan barbecue?" Lola said, grinning.

"Nope. Definitely not another one like that," Christine said, flipping her hair. "It's a celebratory birthday bash." She then spun back toward Tommy and said, "Obviously, we would love to welcome you, as well. You got our girl safely home and in one piece, just a year older."

"A year more raggedy. A year more tired," Lola tried, laughing.

Lola and Tommy still kept away from one another as they unpacked the boat and loaded up the truck. Zach filled the air with plenty of questions, pegged toward Tommy, about the route they had taken both down to the Keys via car and the one back via sailboat. Tommy and Zach created one of those typical male-bonding conversations, with a lot of jargon and a lot of directions, which made Christine, Audrey, and Lola shrug.

"I can't believe you put together a party for me," Lola said as they pulled into the driveway.

"The last year of your thirties is one to celebrate!" Christine pressed open the door and pulled Lola into the house, where they found a wide collection of the Sheridan clan—including Wes, Susan, Scott, Aunt Kerry, Uncle Trevor, cousins Kelli, Charlotte, Claire, Steve, along with all their families, Amanda and her fiancé, Chris, whom Lola had never met (he was handsome and successful and confident, altogether perfect for Amanda), along with Jake,

Susan's eldest, his wife Kristen, and their twin babies, who scampered across the floor and stumbled into random objects. As Lola hugged everyone tight, her best friends Monica and Hannah, along with their families, entered as well. On the porch, Scott sweated over the first round of many burgers and hot dogs and gave a burly wave.

"You've made a huge sacrifice, being the one to barbecue," Lola called from the large gathering of people.

"I can't hear you over the sizzle!" Scott joked back. "The barbecue is where I belong. You know that."

Christine had baked the most delightful lavender and lemon birthday cake, nearly two feet tall, with gorgeous flowers dotted across it. Lola fawned over it as Christine explained this was the cake she had tried to make for Abby and Gail's fifteenth birthday the month before. Nobody had seen it, because Zach had accidently destroyed it.

"I don't know how you ever managed to forgive him for that," Lola said.

"Me neither. I certainly won't let him forget it as long as he lives," Christine said.

Lola wandered onto the porch and watched as her family and friends descended onto the various picnic tables, set up across both the porch and the yard overlooking the water. It was just past seven-thirty, and the sun had begun to dip into a pink haze at the horizon. Looking at it only reminded her of some of the most gorgeous things she had seen out on the open waves.

From down on the grass, she looked up to see that Tommy Gasbarro himself stood on the porch, shaking hands with her father, a beer in-hand. Her heart thudded. Why had Tommy decided to stay for the birthday? Sure, it wasn't like Tommy to turn down free beer, that was for sure, but after their fight the day before, she had thought maybe he wanted nothing to do with her.

Susan approached. Her hand dotted over the top of her glossy red wig, and she gave Lola a weak smile. "How did it go out there?"

Lola tilted her head to-and-fro. "It was weird."

"Weird how?"

"Difficult to explain," Lola offered. "Suffice it to say; I can't believe he's still here. I figured he would kick me off that boat and then sail away as fast as he could."

"You know you're addicting, Lorraine Sheridan. Men can't get enough of you."

"I really don't think that's the case here," Lola returned. "Although that's really sweet to say. Especially as I creep closer and closer to forty."

"Ha. Forty was eons ago for me," Susan said. "But, I do remember when I hit thirty-nine, how weird that number was."

"Because of Mom."

"Because of Mom," Susan echoed. "Especially out there on the water."

"I couldn't stop thinking about her. Not for a second. The worst is that my memories of her are pretty foggy, you know? I was eleven. I hadn't even hit puberty yet. I liked to climb trees and play with dolls. And then, one day, my mom never came home, and one by one, my sisters left me."

Susan breathed a sigh. "You know I'll never forgive myself for it. For any of it."

"I know. But you should. I don't mean to linger on it. I'm just nostalgic. I'm worried that if I stay on the Vineyard for the rest of my life, I'll always have to stare at the past non-stop, rather than moving beyond it. You know?"

"I know the fear," Susan affirmed. "I thought it, too, when I considered staying here, making a life with Scott. But the fact is we're Vineyard girls. I feel Mom in every room of this house, including the new ones. I hear Mom in the stories Dad tells us, even as they become fewer and farther between. I want to cling to what matters. And you're part of that, sis."

"Thank you," Lola said. Tears swelled in her eyes as she hugged Susan. When she drew back, she turned to find that Scott had joined the gathering of Tommy, Wes, and Zach. "I can't believe it. Look how he fits in with them."

"Didn't you say he was a loner?" Susan asked.

"He definitely is," Lola replied. "I think he's just trying on the role of family-man."

"Hmm. It suits him," Susan returned. "I'm going to go check on the snacks, make sure nothing needs to be refilled. You want to come get a glass of wine?"

"More than anything," Lola admitted.

She followed Susan up the porch steps, past Tommy and the other men, then back into the house. Christine stood with Amanda, Charlotte, and Charlotte's daughter, Rachel, talking about Amanda's upcoming wedding. Amanda said she wanted to wait for her mother to find the perfect dress. At this, Susan teased, saying, "I thought you always said you wanted to wear my dress, honey?"

Amanda laughed. "I always said that until I realized a late-'90s look doesn't really cut it anymore."

"It was very stylish back in the day," Susan laughed. "And you were just the cutest little flower girl!"

"That's right! You didn't marry until after your children were born," Charlotte said. "I always forget that. When we got your card in the mail with the news of your first baby, I totally screamed. You had Jake at, what. Nineteen?"

"Yes. I think Richard almost high-tailed it when it happened," Susan said, uncorking a bottle of wine and pouring several glasses. "No matter what happened later, he did stick around for all the diapers, feedings, teethings and— worst of all—the teenage years. I can't hate him for that."

"Although I can hate Penelope all day long," Amanda grumbled, rolling her eyes.

"Don't," Susan said. "She's just a confused girl who's going to wake up one day and realize she married a guy twenty years older than her, who likes to go to bed around nine-thirty."

"Sad," Charlotte said.

"Penelope loves Instagram and forced my dad to set up an account," Amanda said mischievously. "Do you want to see?"

"Yes!" Christine cried.

"Good grief." Susan shook her head and passed a glass of white wine to Lola.

"Look," Amanda said, drawing up the lone image Richard had posted—a half-selfie of himself and one of the local beers he apparently liked. The selfie was the kind only an awkward dad could take, a little too close to the cheeks, making them appear monstrous.

"That's really bad," Christine laughed.

"Richard's a criminal lawyer," Susan said. "Not a social media mogul."

"Apparently not anymore," Lola said, grinning.

The party continued deeper into the night. At some point, Christine yanked Lola in front of the birthday cake and everyone sang happy birthday, including Tommy, who stood near the back with Zach. Lola closed her eyes, but she couldn't think of anything to wish for except a healthy baby for Audrey. She blew out the candles quickly, which resulted in mass applause.

"Thank you," she said. "I'll be here all night."

An hour or so later, Scott and Tommy walked together across the porch. They stopped briefly to chat with Susan and Lola, who stood together toward the back of the porch, watching the festivities.

"I'm going to drive Tommy over to Chuck's," Scott announced.

Lola furrowed her brow. "What?"

"He doesn't have a place to stay but needs to be on the Vineyard a little bit longer. The place is completely empty, and I think it makes sense that Tommy stay there," Scott explained.

"Oh, yes! And we owe you, of course, for getting Lola back in one piece," Susan said.

For the first time in over a day, Lola's eyes burned into Tommy's. Why had he agreed to this? Was it really just convenience? Why did he need to stay on the island? Wasn't that big, wide world still out there waiting for him?

"I appreciate it," Tommy said, turning his eyes back toward Susan.

"And let us know if you need anything else," Susan said. "Should I pack some cake for you?"

"No, no. I don't want to intrude any more than I already have," Tommy said.

"Nonsense. How have you intruded?" Susan demanded.

Hurriedly, she cut toward the cake table (normally, the puzzle table) and added several slices to a Tupperware. When she passed it back to him, she said, "And don't worry if you don't remember to return it. I know how these things go."

"I'll do my best to remember," Tommy said.

Again, his eyes turned toward Lola. Lola dropped her gaze to the floor, suddenly afraid. What was it about this guy that completely floored her? Why, after all, they had been through, was he still standing there? Why had he decided to stay at Chuck's place?

"Let me know when the article is published," he finally said. "I look forward to reading it."

With Tupperware in-hand, he turned toward the back door, following after Scott toward the truck Zach and Christine and Audrey had picked them up in. Without Tommy in front of her, Lola's eyes turned toward Audrey, who had stationed herself on the couch with a small plate across her lap, a half-eaten slice of cake on top. The poor girl had fallen asleep; her head tossed over a pillow and her mouth wide open. Beside her, on the other side of the couch, was Wes, in a similar position. Lola chuckled to herself and hurried toward her daughter and her father, grateful to have a job to do.

"Let's get you guys off to bed."

CHAPTER 15

The next morning, after a healthy scrubbing of the kitchen and a nice clean-up of the porch, Lola sat at the picnic table with all her notes from the sailing adventure piled out in front of her. Although her memories had colored the experience a bit, she still felt a pang of excitement as she read over them. On one, she had actually forced Tommy to pose so that she could sketch him. He had thrust out one of his arms, bent it, and then bulged out his bicep muscles to make her laugh. Her sketch didn't do his handsomeness justice.

Throughout the journey, she'd also had time to conduct several interviews with him—about his sailing trips all over the world, about what he loved most about sailing from the Keys to Martha's Vineyard, about the quality of waves in the Atlantic versus the Pacific. Slowly, as she read through her pages of notes, Lola began to cultivate the story of this mystery man. Her fingers found the keyboard of her computer and began to type.

Thomas Gasbarro comes from a long line of explorers. His father, he says, was so invested in the idea of world-domination, that he almost immediately abandoned his mother, moved on to the next woman, and then the next, in the style of a Roman emperor. This is the sort of humor that Tommy Gasbarro brings. Seated with him on his gorgeous vessel as the waves lap up against the sides, I'm mesmerized with him, with his bravery, with his decision to live outside the bounds of a "normal life."

Lola studied the words that had just poured from her fingers. Did she actually feel this way about Tommy? Her heart seemed to glow as she wrote of him.

There's a certain artistry of a sailor in his main environment. It's a fluidity that one hardly gets to see. There's a sense of casual urgency, just as, if it had any thought processes, the heart might illustrate, given that it must pump blood to all areas of our body. In this manner, Tommy Gasbarro is the essential heartbeat of the sailboat. He's able to both tilt the sails and sing an old sea chanty, one he says an old pirate from Cambodia told him. "That pirate had a fascinating story, but so does everyone else in Cambodia. Everyone seems as though they're running from something. I met several people who were running from the American law. Nobody can really track people down in Cambodia. It's not clear why."

As a Martha's Vineyard girl and Boston College grad, I've hardly left New England in my thirty-nine years. His stories sound like reflections of another reality I might have had if I had shifted my course. Still, there's a sense that, with Tommy Gasbarro by your side, your course has a chance of taking you wherever it wants to go. Tommy lets the wind guide him. It's something we all should do more often. It's certainly the most freeing feeling in the world.

Lola grew lost in the writing, so lost that she didn't hear Christine as she crept in from her shift at the bistro and dropped herself onto the picnic table beside Lola. She poured herself a glass of wine and then tried her best to peek over Lola's shoulder to read.

"Not yet! It isn't ready," Lola cried.

"Ugh. Whatever. I can't focus on it, anyway," Christine said. "I'm exhausted from your birthday and waking up so early this morning. Long gone are the days when I could party all night and be a pastry chef in the morning. Hair of the dog it is." She lifted her glass to salute the apparent thud of her head.

"Ha. I'll join you," Lola said. It was just after noon, but it was getting close to the end of summer, and she felt called to drift into another mindset for a moment.

Besides, she needed to hash out everything that had happened between her and Tommy. And she had a hunch that Christine was the one to speak to.

Before she could get started, however, Susan appeared in the screen door. "What are you two doing out here?" she said, creaking it open.

"I didn't know you were home!" Lola said.

"Sure. I just helped Dad set up his puzzle," Susan said. "Another one thousand pieces to put together. He also has the pre-game on for baseball. I would say he's all set up for the day."

Lola rushed up to fetch another two glasses for herself and Susan.

"Where are Audrey and Amanda?" Christine asked.

"I think they went swimming somewhere with a few locals they met," Susan offered. "Probably kids of people we went to school with."

"Did you ask who they were?" Lola asked.

"Sure, but they didn't know last names," Susan added.

"I wonder if Audrey will find a local to fall in love with," Christine said, her voice hushed.

"Don't get my hopes up," Lola said. "Oh! I forgot. I haven't shown you who her baby-daddy is. Here." She grabbed her phone and flashed up that now-familiar photo of Max Gray.

"Wow. He is super handsome," Susan breathed.

"He looks like a grade-A asshole," Christine said. "And I should know. I've dated enough of them."

"Tommy doesn't seem like a grade-A asshole," Susan said, arching her brow.

"There it is. You're sneaking right into the topic you want to know all about," Lola said. "It's always been one of your talents, Susan Sheridan. Admit it."

"I'm a lawyer. Of course, I know that," Susan said, crossing her arms over her chest.

"Come on! Tell us at least one thing about the trip," Christine pleaded. "He stayed at our place for ages last night. It's clear that he likes you."

"I don't know if that's true. Or, if it was true, I don't think it is anymore," Lola said contemplatively. She then continued to explain what had happened on her birthday, how he'd told that story about the SAT test, how she had freaked out.

"You almost died in a storm on your birthday. I think you acted exactly how you should have," Susan said, her eyes as big as saucers.

"I mean, that's the thing. We probably didn't almost die," Lola said. "It was just too eerily similar to the thing with Stan. But Tommy took offense to it. And he accused me of only hanging out with him because he's a part of the past I'm trying to piece together. So, yeah. You could say it was all a disaster. We're not even speaking right now."

The sisters all sipped their wine slowly, unsure of what to say next.

"I hate it when I get my hopes up about someone and they let me down," Christine stated.

"I kind of thought there was something special about him. That's for sure," Lola said. "And there is. Really, there is. But I think he's too much of a loner to ever be with me or with anyone. Even though he's still on the island, it's not like he'll stick around for long. He told me all these stories of sailing the open seas all over the world. He's a mystery man. He's like Ernest Hemingway mixed with Captain Balboa. He probably wouldn't be into, like, sleeping with one woman in the same bed every single night."

Susan and Christine struggled to give her any advice. Christine mentioned that she seemed to understand the situation much better than they ever could, and also that she was just so sorry about it all. Susan said she had only ever been with two men, basically, and couldn't fully imagine waging the war of "dating" into her thirties and forties. "Both of you are much braver than me," she said. "Thank God, Scott wanted me back. What would I do? Join Tinder?"

This brightened Lola's mood, albeit only slightly. "Tinder is actually fantastic," she said. "I had a lot of fun in my early thirties with that. Especially once Audrey had sleepovers and friends and even boyfriends, things that kept her busy and out of the house. I met some wild guys. Always fun. Nobody I ever wanted Audrey to meet."

"I did OKCupid for a while," Christine admitted, her cheeks reddening.

"And now you're with your high school enemy," Susan said, brimming with joy. "Weird how life goes, isn't it?"

"The weirdest," Christine said.

Lola's phone buzzed on the table. She blinked down from her wine haze to see that Colin had sent her an email.

"Ah! I saw the slightest smile out of you," Susan said, pointing.

"It's not a big deal," Lola said. "Just my editor. Colin."

"The guy who's in love with you," Christine said.

"Audrey really can't shut up about that, can she?" Lola said.

She scanned the email. Colin reported that he was excited to read her newest article about Tommy Gasbarro; that he was glad she'd arrived back to Martha's Vineyard safely. He also said that he planned to come to Martha's Vineyard soon for a visit.

"Would you mind showing me around?" he wrote.

"He's coming to the Vineyard," Lola said, unsure of how she felt about it.

"Wow. That's incredible!" Christine said.

"I guess." Lola's heart felt heavy from the Tommy experience. Still, she knew that it was better to press forward to try out people the way you might try out sweaters at a retail store. Some of them were scratchy, irritating, or hung wrong; others fit just right.

CHAPTER 16

It was pretty clear what Colin's intentions were the second he stepped off that boat.

He looked handsome: clean-cut, jeans that suited his taut and muscular frame, a bright-toothed smile that immediately exploded the second he spotted Lola on the dock. He carried only a light backpack since he planned to only stay one night, and he strutted so casually toward her, like a football player on his way from practice. Lola should know. She had dated quite a bit of the football team, mostly as a joke to herself. She had always been too artistic for them.

"What a gorgeous day," Colin said as a greeting. He beamed at her. For a split second, Lola thought he might drop down and give her a kiss.

She was grateful he didn't.

"Did you have a good trip?" she asked.

"Yes. I haven't been on a boat in ages," Colin said. "I can't believe you grew up here. Right in this town?"

"Yep, here in Oak Bluffs," Lola said. They turned away from the ferry and joined the swarm of tourists. "I thought maybe we would head to my family's Inn for some breakfast before we do some hiking and sight-seeing. What do you think?"

"I think my day is in your hands, and I wouldn't want it anywhere else," Colin said.

Lola had the funniest feeling that her smile was false, that it was made of plastic and about to stretch too far. She forced herself to fall into familiar banter. They spoke about the piece she had just submitted the day before, which Colin adored.

"I think it's one of the best things you've ever written, period," Colin told her. He placed his hands on the tablecloth at the Sunrise Cove Inn bistro and studied her contemplatively. "I honestly think it could win a few awards if we submit it. But beyond that..."

Suddenly, Christine appeared at the table. She beamed at both of them, then placed a basket of croissants in front of them. "Good morning!"

"Good morning," Colin began. "I'm afraid I haven't looked at the menu yet."

"This is actually my sister, Colin. Christine."

"Ah! The middle one," Colin said. "What a delight to meet you." He stretched out his hand and shook hers.

"You as well! I guess you've spent the better part of ten years with my little sister, so I'm sure you have a lot of stories," Christine said. "Oh. And regardless of the menu, I have to say, the new pineapple mimosa we have on special right now is to die for. If you're looking to drink at ten in the morning, that is."

"I'm on vacation," Colin said, chuckling. "And a mimosa sounds like a dream. Lola?"

"You know I'm always down," Lola said.

Christine disappeared behind the kitchen door again. Lola blinked up again at Colin, who'd never forgotten when he was interrupted and always returned exactly to the subject he'd left off on.

"Where was I? Oh, yes. Your article. It pains me to say this, but I really think you should embark to other, more prosperous publications after this," he continued. "You have such a stunning resume after all this, and there's no reason you shouldn't be writing for the New York Times or even submitting to travel magazines about life on Martha's Vineyard."

"Ha. National Geographic—life on a bougie island," Lola teased.

Colin laughed good-naturedly. "Something like that. I know it must be complicated for you right now, rejoining your family on the island and figuring out what's next. But if you need help finding another publication, sending resumes and cover letters, know that I will help you with it all. Every step of the way."

Lola studied his eager face. On the one hand, it was very attractive to have someone so interested in her or, as Audrey and Christine said, "in love." On the other, there was something she didn't trust about it. They had been friends for ten years after deciding they weren't a good fit. Why, then, had he changed his tune?

"Thank you, Colin. I appreciate that," she told him, her nostrils flared.

They ordered mimosas from the server. Colin bit into the

crunchy exterior of Christine's gift to the earth, considered it for a moment, and then said, "They're great. Almost as good as that bakery in East Boston. The one by your old apartment. Remember, we used to get them around ten years ago? Smeared them with butter and added cheese? Man, I miss my late-twenties metabolism."

Lola appreciated the memory, but she resented his saying that Christine's was second to anyone. She remembered her manners and played along, saying, "That place, unfortunately, closed down, I think around four years ago. I liked it, too. The owner was sweet. It was a little old lady whose husband had just died, so she opened a bakery. It was her life's dream."

"You always find the story, don't you?" Colin said.

"I guess it's my job," Lola said with a shrug.

Again, he beamed at her. There was a kernel of doubt that seemed to grow stronger in Lola's stomach. *He'll only be here one day,* she told herself. She could make it one day.

After a breakfast of eggs benedict and two pineapple mimosas, Lola led Colin into the Sunrise Cove Inn lobby to greet Natalie and Wes, who now manned the lobby desk together. This was to allow Wes to feel involved in everyday operations at the Inn, despite his occasional bouts of confusion.

"Hello, Lola!" her father said brightly.

"Hey, Dad," Lola said. "This is my friend, Colin, from Boston. We've known each other for a long time. Colin, this is my dad."

Colin and Wes shook hands. Wes studied him for a moment, maintaining a smile that, to Lola's eyes, seemed a bit plastic, like hers.

"Welcome to Martha's Vineyard!" he said. "It's good you came now, at the end of August. We're all squeezing the last bit of summer out of it."

"Does every door slam shut on September first?" Colin asked.

"Just about," Lola affirmed. "We're going to go hiking and swimming for a bit. See you later? Oh, and Natalie. You reserved Colin's single room for him, didn't you? The one with the ocean view?"

Natalie blinked at the little ledge before her and nodded briskly. "Yep! Here it is. I can take your backpack up to the room if you like?"

"That's okay. I didn't pack much," Colin said. "Just the key, I guess."

Natalie placed the key on the counter between them. Colin gave Lola a strange glance. She suspected the look was confusion, above everything else. He had come all this way, and she didn't plan to stay with him? He'd come all this way, and she had gotten him a single room?

Still, it wasn't like she owed him anything. She had to stay true to that.

Whatever awkwardness that had formed between them dissipated quickly, Lola grabbed one of the Inn cars and hopped into the front seat, watching as Colin boarded and clicked his seatbelt into place.

"I read a little bit about that Flying Horses Carousel," Colin said, as Lola cranked the engine. "I had no idea it was first located in New York City before moving to Martha's Vineyard in the 1890s."

"Actually, it was the 1880s. Close, though," Lola said.

"Ha. Thanks for the correction. But it's the oldest operating platform carousel in America? And it still has those old brass rings that you can try to grab as you ride around," Colin continued.

"Sure does," Lola affirmed, wondering why this guy felt it was necessary to mansplain something that literally existed in the town she had grown up in, something she'd ridden probably four thousand times before the age of ten. "Cool that you looked it up."

"Oh! And Oak Bluffs used to be called Cottage City," Colin continued.

"Yep..."

"Sorry. Ha. I went down a pretty deep Wikipedia hole last night," Colin said. "You know how I get excited about facts."

"I get it," Lola said, choosing to laugh.

Despite her annoyance at him, Lola still wanted to impress him. She drove them westward, all the way to the Aquinnah Cliffs Overlook. Once they had parked, he walked, dumbstruck, toward the edge of the cliffs and blinked out across the gorgeous crystal waters. After a long pause, he said, "I don't have any facts about this."

Finally, Lola felt herself muster a genuine laugh for maybe the first time that day.

"Naw. It's extraordinary," Colin said. He spread his arms out on either side of him, letting the wind rustle through his clean shirt.

At this moment, Lola couldn't help but think of Tommy— shirtless and a tiny bit dirty on board the sailboat. What a contrast they were. Colin was the kind of man who wanted the life she did; Tommy was the kind of man she wanted.

They walked down the coast a bit until they got to the beach. They both walked away in separate bushes and changed into their swimsuits, then rushed into the waves. Lola screeched like a child at the chilly water, while Colin laughed wildly and swept toward her, making his knees pop up out of the water as he splashed. Lola splashed him back and, for a split-second, again, she thought— maybe? Maybe him? But within a few moments, he had explained to her the history of whaling on the island, and again, she found herself rolling her eyes.

Of course, she knew about the island's history of whaling.

"Have you ever seen a whale?" she asked him.

He shook his head, despondently. "You know that I grew up in Ohio, right? We don't have much going on there. Cornfields and soybean fields and... Hmm."

"Come on. We went there together. It was beautiful," Lola said. "It was so green!"

"Sure. But it's no Martha's Vineyard."

"Well, fortunately, not everything is," Lola agreed.

After they went for a swim, Lola and Colin hiked around the area for a bit then plopped down by the water to enjoy a bit of wine. Colin told her more about some of the events back in the city —friends she missed, the fact that the construction had finally cleared, that sort of thing.

"The city really is different without you, Lola," Colin said. He gave her that look again—that glow-eyed, hopeful look. "Maybe for a while you could consider doing half-time? The city for a week, the island for a week. That sort of thing?"

"Maybe," Lola said doubtfully. "Although, I think I told you,

Audrey is pregnant, and I want to be around for as much of it as I can."

"Audrey is literally from Boston," Colin said with a laugh. "I can't imagine she wouldn't want to come back with you."

"And my father. He has dementia. And Christine, she's just started at the bakery, and..."

Colin raised a flat palm. "Just think about it. Maybe you would be happier with the best of both worlds."

Lola resented being told that she wasn't happy already. The moment she opened her lips to tell him, however, a large seagull squawked overhead, and Colin was suddenly ripe with seagull facts.

Lola was very close to calling it a day, faking a headache. Maybe stumbling on a rock and feigning a major injury. Anything. But when she thought really hard about it, she forced herself to stop. Colin was a friend; he would understand when the time came and she told him the truth. At least, she hoped he would.

Colin and Lola grabbed dinner in Edgartown, so he could see that side of the island and then drove back toward the Sunrise Cove Inn that evening as the sun set. As the Inn turned into view, Lola's heart thudded with fear. She hoped and prayed that Colin wouldn't make some sort of pass and ask her to come upstairs with him.

As they parked out front, Colin nodded toward the side of the Inn and said, "Hey. Isn't that your sailor?"

Lola felt like all the wind had been knocked out of her. Tommy stood alongside the Inn with Scott, as Scott pointed up to a few spare boards that had come undone from the side of the building. Tommy held a hammer in one of his large hands, and he wore a white undershirt that highlighted his muscles incredibly. He looked like a painting of the first man.

"Um. Yep," Lola said, totally confused.

"I didn't think I'd get to meet him! You said in the article that he was always on the move, so I assumed he would be gone," Colin said.

"Me too, I guess," Lola returned.

"Come on. Introduce me," Colin said.

"He looks pretty busy."

"We're giving him loads of publicity. I think he owes it to me," Colin said.

"He didn't even want publicity," Lola offered, all the while remembering that she had only agreed to go on that trip, to write the piece, because she had wanted to get closer to him. She had wanted to get as close to her subject as possible.

Now, he seemed like a stranger.

Colin strode across the grass toward Tommy and Scott. Lola stalled behind him. It was like watching a car crash. As they approached, Scott turned around. His eyes scanned over toward Lola.

"Hey there!" he said, all smiles. "Susan said you had a friend in town? I guess this must be him."

Tommy looked moody and stoic as Lola gestured and said, "Yeah, this is my editor and good friend, Colin. Colin, this is Scott, my sister's boyfriend—both in high school and now—and Tommy, um, the sailor I went on that trip with."

Tommy's eyes were just as stormy as they had been that last day on the boat.

"Good to meet you, man," Colin said, sticking out his hand toward Tommy.

Tommy gripped it and shook exactly once. He dropped Colin's hand like it was a toy. "Hello," he said.

"A man of few words," Colin said. He looked jittery. "I just read Lola's article about you. I'm about to press publish. You know what? I think it's one of her best."

"I assume that she did a good job. She's a professional journalist," Tommy said. The words were flat, without a single scent of congratulations.

"Yes, true. Very true. I just think she brought a bit of color and life to the article that maybe another journalist wouldn't have," Colin said.

"Good to hear. Pleases me to know thousands of strangers might get a good sense of who I really am as a person," Tommy returned.

The sarcasm was so palpable, Lola was surprised Colin didn't choke on it.

"Cool, man. Really cool," Colin said. "Well, I guess I'd better get up to my room. Lola, you want to see me inside?"

Lola nodded. "Sure thing. Good to see you both."

Before Tommy or Scott could answer, Lola, followed Colin into the lobby. By the time they reached the interior, Colin had already said, "There's just something about those guys who spend too much time alone, you know? They're so lonely that they don't even know how to make small talk. It irritates me."

Lola said goodbye not long after that. Colin was clearly a bit frustrated with that, but also said he'd had a wonderful day. She suggested they have coffee and croissants before he had to catch the ferry the next morning, and he agreed whole-heartedly his smile widening. He then hugged her a little too tightly, then freed her like a bird from a cage.

By the time she got back outside, neither Scott nor Tommy was anywhere in sight. Her heart beat dully, as though she swam somewhere deep underwater.

CHAPTER 17

THE NEXT MORNING AT BREAKFAST WITH COLIN, LOLA PICKED through a croissant slowly, insisting that she wasn't hungry enough for a full breakfast, and listened to Colin rattle off the rest of his summer plans. At various junctures, he paused, as though he waited for her to interject that she wanted to be a part of those plans, too. Lola didn't say anything. She didn't want to hurt him. But she did want him gone.

After she dropped Colin off at the ferry, Lola leaped into an Inn vehicle and drove like a maniac down County Road, turning left at Edgartown-Vineyard Haven Road without a single inkling of what she wanted to do or where she wanted to go. She crept more and more toward Edgartown, then turned south toward Norton Point Beach. Before she fully knew what she had done, she parked the car next to The Right Fork Diner, a traditional American diner with the slogan, "Just Good Plane Food!" since it had views that overlooked the airfields. As she'd only managed to eat through one-half of a croissant, due to nerves, Lola had cooked herself up a decent appetite. She wanted to sit at a table, all by herself, and gaze out the window. She didn't want to hear a single Wikipedia factoid for the rest of the day.

Lola ordered the Crabby Eggs Benedict, with seared crab cake and hollandaise sauce, along with a mimosa. As she returned the menu to the server, she once again had to admit, "Yes, I'm one of the Sheridan sisters. Yep, the youngest one, Lola."

The woman, approximately her age in a bright red apron, tilted her hips and said, "Isn't that just the way? We all find a way to come home, don't we?"

Lola was accustomed to eating alone, especially after so many on-location trips for her career. She dug into her meal and stared ahead with somber eyes. The radio station played music from the early 'oos, back when Audrey had been a little thing and eager to jump around and dance in their combined living room and kitchenette. Britney Spears, Justin Timberlake, J.Lo. Lola smirked at the memory, at the strange fashions—the bellbottoms she had worn on purpose over pairs of stiletto heels and the neon pink, so much neon pink, which she'd eventually given away in bulk at a church rummage sale down the block.

When Lola finished eating, she paid and tipped big, then left her car in the lot to wander south toward Katama Beach, which was a large and long peninsula of sand down on the south-eastern-most point on the island, a region with Katama Bay on the northern side and the Atlantic on the other. There, Katama Beach became Norton Point Beach, which then became Edgartown South Beach. Lola yanked off her shoes and walked slowly down the beach, digging her toes in the sand. Although it was still tourist season, the numbers had dwindled in the past week—proof that, in just a few days' time, September would peek her ugly head through the calendar window.

Lola walked for what felt like forever until she reached the eastern tip of the peninsula that held full views of the neighboring Chappaquiddick Island. There on that point, she closed her eyes, inhaled softly, slowly.

There, as she stood with the breeze across her cheeks, she knew the full answer to the Colin equation.

He wasn't the one for her.

She would find no happiness in his arms.

With this final admission, Lola allowed her shoulders to droop. She supposed, in a sense, she had wanted to return to Audrey with the news that she'd had a "much better time" than she'd anticipated; she wanted the hope that was tied up in a new relationship, a person who genuinely cared and wanted to be there.

Still, if there was anything Lola was and had always been, it was true to herself, to her heart, to her ideals.

Lola returned to Oak Bluffs about an hour later. She parked in the driveway and cut out of the car. Immediately, she heard the familiar, sing-song voices of Audrey and Wes out on the porch that overlooked the Sound. Her heart grew warm. As she stepped inside, she recognized that her father informed Audrey about the various types of birds that he normally spotted, even just in the woods near the house.

"The birds I like the most, I think, are the White-Throated Sparrows," Wes explained. "They've got such interesting faces. Oh!

And the European Starlings. Goodness, Audrey, you really must go with me some time."

Lola reached for a glass of water and filled it, as Audrey responded with, "Why don't we go right now?"

"Fantastic. I'll grab my hat and binoculars," Wes returned.

Suddenly, both Wes and Audrey appeared in the dark haze of the inner room. Audrey blinked toward her mother, recognizing her only after her eyes adjusted.

"How did it go with Colin!" she asked, as Wes disappeared in the closet in the far hallway. "You were so guarded last night."

"Um. It was okay," Lola said with a shrug.

"Just okay?" Audrey said, sounding disappointed. "But I was right about why he came, wasn't I?"

Lola rolled her eyes playfully. "Yes, Audrey. You were right."

"I knew it," Audrey said.

After Wes reappeared with binoculars and two hats, he dropped one atop Audrey's head and beamed at her. "I've got myself a new partner, Lola. What do you think about that?"

"Finally, time for Audrey to get a new hobby," Lola teased.

In reality, Lola knew that this particular weekend was difficult for Audrey. All the other students returned to Penn State, to their houses and dorms, to their parties and lives. Not Audrey, though. She would stay on the Vineyard for another two semesters, have her baby, nurse the baby, and then when the time was right, return to Penn State—assuredly with a baby-sized hole in her heart.

Lola knew that the separation would be difficult for Audrey. It very well could rip her in two.

As Audrey followed Wes back out onto the porch, she spun back and added, "I guess Colin's no Tommy Gasbarro, huh?"

Lola grumbled. "Maybe it's time you stay out of my love life? Unless you want me to get involved with yours."

"Point taken," Audrey affirmed. "Catch you later."

Lola situated herself on the porch swing with a mug of tea and blinked out across the Sound. Her thoughts were hazy, inarticulate. It felt strange to be alone at the big house alone, especially after that summer—and it made her jumpy and a bit volatile, as though she had lost touch with the idea of being with her thoughts.

The screen door swung closed to reveal Christine, bleary-eyed and in the middle of a yawn.

"There you are!" she said. "Susan and Scott are on their way here. Susan says she has an appetite for the first time in a few days and wants to grill. You game?"

"Sure thing," Lola said. "I'll start the coals if you pour the wine?"

"Always," Christine returned.

Lola got to work, grateful to have something to do with her hands. As she fired up the coals, Christine chatted about her day at the bistro, about how school was about to start, which meant that Ronnie would have to take fewer hours, and about working fewer hours, herself, now that the bistro would transition into autumn.

"To be honest, working six days a week at the bistro has nearly destroyed me," Christine said. "I'll be glad to sleep in a little bit more. Drink coffee on the porch after eight instead of after four."

"You deserve it," Lola said.

Felix stuck his head up on the screen window. Christine let the little creature out on the porch. He sauntered out like he owned the place. Even his meows sounded like orders.

"He's really taken to the Vineyard," Lola said with a laugh.

"I know. It's like he always had it in him," Christine said.

Scott and Susan arrived a few minutes later with groceries. Susan's skin looked a bit brighter; her eyes seemed clear. Still, she sat on the porch swing next to Lola and gripped her arm with exhaustion.

"I missed you! You played host all day yesterday, and I hardly saw you a second," Susan said.

"Oh, right. Your editor," Scott said. "He seemed like a decent guy?"

"He's all right," Lola admitted. After a pause, she said, "I see that Tommy's helping you with some Inn repairs?"

Scott nodded. "He's been a big help, actually."

Lola felt as though Scott didn't want to give her all the information she needed.

It was also possible that he wasn't being secretive on purpose. Men were a little oblivious like that, weren't they?

"I'm just surprised he's still there," Lola continued, watching as Scott removed the burger meat and hot dogs from the crinkly paper bag. Lola gripped the stem of her wine glass a little too hard; her fingers turned white.

"Yeah?" Scott said.

"Yeah. Still, at Chuck's, I mean. I had a feeling that he wouldn't stick around so long."

Scott disappeared for a moment, then reappeared with a large plate and several containers of spices. He then washed his hands and returned to the porch to begin to prepare the meat. All the while, the Sheridan sisters remained quiet.

Finally, Susan aided Lola's quest along.

"Why did he stick around so long, Scott?" she asked.

"Hmm? Oh. Tommy?"

"Yes. Gosh," Christine said, snapping back into old-world, volatile Christine.

Scott blinked, clearly confused. "Oh, um. He mentioned something about needing to stick around on the Vineyard because of erm. Of Stan." He dropped his eyes back to the meat and began to knead spices into the pink meat.

Ah! So he had been cagey on purpose.

He hadn't wanted to say Stan's name and get the Sheridan sisters all riled up.

But here they were: riled up.

"What's up with Stan?" Lola interjected.

Scott's cheeks burned red. "He um. He's had some health problems lately, apparently."

"Oh my gosh," Susan blurted. "I just realized. I haven't seen Stan Ellis out on his boat in weeks."

"That's so true! Normally, no matter where you are on the island, if you look out—you see Stan and his little fishing boat," Christine said.

"He must be really sick," Susan marveled. "I can't believe we didn't notice it until now."

"I think we've had enough on our plate to notice," Christine said.

Everyone held this thought for a moment. Scott splashed various burger patties onto the grill and then placed his hands on his hips. The smell of cooking meat hung in the air.

"It's funny, isn't it?" Christine said then.

"What?" Lola asked.

"Mom came to hate the Inn in the end, right? She said it

represented everything that had gone wrong in her marriage. She wanted to escape all of it and run to Stan. Now, years and years later, Stan Ellis's ex-stepson is the one helping Scott fix it back up again. What a strange series of events. I just wonder what Mom would say about it all."

Suddenly, Wes appeared through the screen door. Apparently, he had arrived back from bird watching with Audrey, and they had entered through the back door to dispose of their shoes in the mudroom. His eyes scanned each of them, and his face was stoic, his eyes stormy.

It was clear that he had been listening. This hadn't been a conversation that any of them had truly wanted him to hear.

"I can tell you what your mother would have said about it all," Wes boomed.

This was a surprise.

"Dad, it's okay. You don't have to talk about this," Susan said. She patted the space beside her on the porch swing, trying to guide him to rest.

"No. I won't sit. I need to say this," Wes continued as his eyes flashed wickedly. "You think it's strange this man helps Scott with the Inn? I think your mother would think it was the simplest thing in the world. Here on Martha's Vineyard, we are about kindness and compassion. We help one another when times are rough. It doesn't matter about the past or where we're headed in the future. If something needs fixing, we fix it. If something needs care, we give it. And if someone needs forgiving, we forgive."

Wes set his jaw and gripped the side of the screen door with white knuckles. Audrey appeared beside him, the binoculars still strapped around her neck. After a strange pause, her eyes cut across the crowd, searching each of their faces.

"If I'm not mistaken, I think I just walked into yet another awkward Sheridan conversation," she said. "What did you guys step in this time?"

CHAPTER 18

Lola stirred in her thoughts about Tommy for the next several days. On the morning of September 2, she yanked up in bed, no longer able to sleep, and blinked up at the strange Third Eye Blind poster she had hung on the wall as a teenager. She had declared Kevin Cardogan the hottest man to ever live, something both Monica and Hannah had taken issue with. They'd had countless arguments about it in that very bedroom: three bright and frantic teenagers, ready to take on the world. Now, she was thirty-nine and on the brink of something else. Middle age? New love? A better career? She reached up to adjust the folded-over corner of the glossy poster and shuddered with fear.

Summer felt over. Clouds had been called on-duty and hung low in the sky as Lola sipped her coffee with Wes, who seemed disinterested in his puzzle and instead swept a hand over Felix's back and studied the waves.

"What will you do today, Dad?" Lola asked.

"Kerry mentioned something about getting lunch," he said. "Maybe with Claire and the twins over by the flower shop. You want to come?"

Lola agreed if only to escape the nagging of her computer, which sizzled and popped with non-stop emails from Colin—suggestions for new articles, some of which required a visit to Boston. She didn't want to ghost him, exactly; she just wanted more distance, more mental clarity.

At lunch that afternoon, Abby and Gail giggled as they talked to Lola about their first year of high school, which had only just begun. As fifteen-year-old freshmen, they were doe-eyed and fast-moving, speaking excitedly about upcoming football games and homecoming dances and whether or not they would really manage to pass algebra.

"You'd better pass algebra," Claire said, arching her brow. "Or you can forget about carrying those smartphones around."

"These are just problems I never had to deal with when you girls were growing up," Wes said.

"You did have your own problems, though," Aunt Kerry laughed. "Everyone knew you had your hands full. Especially with Miss Lola." She reached across the table playfully and grabbed Lola's wrist.

Abby and Gail grinned at Lola conspiratorially, as though she held the secrets to what it meant to be a worthy teenager. Lola, who had only come to the lunch to escape her own frantic thoughts, felt inarticulate and just laughed.

"Just make sure you pass algebra. Then you can do whatever you want," she said, words that ultimately disappointed the girls.

That evening, as Christine, Wes, and Audrey sat out on the

back porch, Lola paced in her bedroom. The sun had begun to drift toward the horizon, casting a ghoulish, early-autumn glow across everything. Lola felt as though she'd lost too much time.

Suddenly, she grabbed her purse, checked her reflection a final time, then shot down the stairs. She hollered toward the back porch that she would be home in a bit, but didn't wait for any questions. With a flash of her hand, she grabbed the car keys and trotted toward the driveway.

Lola knew the route to Chuck's place since she'd had to drop something off there once before Chuck's epic departure. She drove slowly down the bumpy, unpaved road and then cranked up the little hill that served as the driveway, parking next to a truck that Tommy had probably rented for his time on the island.

Lola's entire body shook with fear. What was that expression she had always told herself as a younger person? *Feel the fear and do it anyway.* Maybe that's what she should have told Abby and Gail at lunch. No matter what scares you, if it thrills you, then do it. Live as much as you can.

Lola walked up the rickety steps of Chuck's house. There was a single orange light coming from the back, along with a fuzzy sound that sounded like a radio or television. Lola lifted her hand toward the wood of the door, but before she could smack it, the door ripped open to reveal the burly sailor, Tommy Gasbarro himself. His eyes were dark, cloudy. Just as she opened her lips to speak, he pressed a finger to his mouth and said, "You have to be quiet."

This wasn't what Lola had expected.

She furrowed her brow and walked inside as Tommy beckoned. Her senses were on fire. Tommy wore a pair of dark jeans and a dark t-shirt, loose at the waist, which hugged his muscles beautifully. His black hair seemed a bit longer than it had out on the boat, and he flipped it back now, gesturing toward the refrigerator.

"Can I get you a beer?"

Lola continued to give him a look of complete and utter confusion.

Finally, Tommy gestured toward the closed door toward the other side of the kitchen area. "Stan is here. I picked him up from minor surgery this afternoon, and he just needs someone around to care for him for a few days. Since Chuck's place is bigger than his place, it had to be here."

Lola's lips formed a round O. She blinked at the wooden door between herself and the man who'd killed her mother. He lay there, asleep, unconscious to the world he'd changed forever. Unconscious to the fact that Anna Sheridan's youngest daughter stood out in the kitchen, wanting nothing more than to barge in and demand of him, *How dare you ruin my life?*

When Lola turned her eyes back toward Chuck, however, she thought better of her instincts. Anna and Stan's accident had happened in 1993. Another summer had come and gone. And there Lola stood, after so much time, after so much space. She nodded and whispered, "Actually, a beer sounds great. Thanks, Tommy."

Tommy grabbed them both Bud Lights and then led her toward the back room, where he snapped off a baseball game and sat in what seemed to be Chuck's main "sports-watching" chair. Lola sat across from him in a rickety rocking chair. The air between them felt strained, just as it had that last day out to sea. How could she explain to him that she wanted to fix whatever this was? How could she ask him for anything beyond what he'd already given?

Shut up, Lola. You haven't even kissed.

"How have you been?" Lola finally asked. It sounded like the most sterile, most boring question in the world.

"Just fine, thanks."

"Has it killed you to be in one place for so long?" she asked then. "I'm sure you're itching to get out of here."

Tommy shrugged. "Stan needs help. He's one of the only people I really care about in the world. Guess it behooves me to stay. Plus, Scott's been really kind, letting me stay here. He says he has no real use for the place since his brother is on the loose. I couldn't believe that story when he told it to me—to go behind so many people's backs on this island. You have to have a real hatred for the people who care about you the most."

Lola swallowed, shocked at his sincerity. Tommy drank a bit of his beer and studied her face. Normally, when faced with a member of the male gender, Lola was able to jump and bound from conversation to conversation. Tommy made her tongue feel glued.

Finally, she forced herself to press forward.

"Listen, Tommy. I've been thinking," she said.

Tommy didn't change his face. He waited, a portrait of solitude and patience.

"I've been thinking that it was really unfair to say some of the things I said when we were on the boat together." Lola exhaled. "I know you've made all your decisions for a reason. You like your life. You aren't a loner because you're afraid of anything. You have made adult, purposeful decisions, and I respect them. Also..." She cupped her knee with the hand that didn't grip her beer. Her heart thudded loudly. "To be honest with you, Tommy, you scare me. You do link up with my past in a very strange way—a way I have to grapple with—but there's also something else about you. Something that makes me think that maybe, I've been looking for you for a really long time. That has nothing to do with my mother or with Stan or with anyone else on this island. It only has to do with you."

Tommy's eyes bore into Lola's. Outside, night had fallen almost completely, and the last of the summertime fireflies blared their light at the tree line. Unlike most of the houses Lola frequented, Chuck's place didn't have an ocean view. It was tucked away in the forest, surrounded by solitude.

"I guess I just. I wanted to tell you that," Lola said finally, acknowledging the silence.

Tommy placed his beer on the coffee table beside him. "A lot of what you said about me is correct."

"But it was so impolite," Lola interjected.

"It doesn't matter. There's no such thing as politeness out on the water," Tommy said. "And in a lot of ways, I appreciated the honesty. It's true that I haven't wanted to settle down with anyone. I haven't seen any reason to build relationships or grow roots. I've just felt rough around the edges. Unwilling to fix myself for anyone."

"I wouldn't want you to fix anything," Lola murmured.

This shut him up for a moment. Again, they regarded one another. Lola leaned forward, then crossed a leg over her knee. She had that strange and urgent desire—to go over to him, to kiss him. To take what she wanted.

"What about that editor of yours?" Tommy asked.

"What about him?"

"I could tell. The way he looked at you, I could tell."

"And what about what I think of him?" Lola returned. "Doesn't that have anything to do with it?"

Tommy opened his lips to speak. At that moment, however, there was a strange jangling coming from the front door, as though someone tried to open the lock. Quick as a flash, Tommy and Lola rushed toward the kitchen and watched as the doorknob turned. The door creaked open—only slightly—until light flashed through the crack from a flashlight.

"What the..." A voice muttered.

"Who's there?" Tommy called.

Lola was petrified. But who would drive all the way out to the middle of the woods to rob a little cabin? It wasn't like Chuck, Tommy, or Stan had anything decent to steal. None of the plates matched; the pots and pans looked like hand-me-downs. One of the table legs was crooked.

Whoever had been on the porch was spooked. He shot down the steps as Tommy and Lola rushed across the rest of the kitchen. Tommy whipped open the door so that he and Lola could see the potential robber as he rushed toward the driveway, where a truck had been parked.

If Lola wasn't mistaken, the man who rushed as quickly as he could away from them was actually the owner of the very cabin in which they stood.

Chuck Frampton had returned.

And they couldn't let him go.

CHAPTER 19

"WHAT THE HECK?" TOMMY BLARED, AS THEY WATCHED Chuck bolt toward the truck at the end of the driveway.

"That's Chuck, Tommy," Lola said. She grabbed his bicep and squeezed hard. "We have to follow him. He stole forty thousand dollars from the Inn, and so much more from other properties around the Vineyard. Susan and Scott have been after him for..."

"Let' go," Tommy said, his eyes darkening. He lurched toward the counter and grabbed the keys to his rental. "Let's go after him."

Lola and Tommy burst out onto the front porch. The moon hung low and its luminescence glow danced across the tip-tops of the trees. Chuck cranked the engine of his truck and tore down the driveway. As Lola cranked into the passenger seat of Tommy's rental, she cried, "I guess that was the surprise of his life. Finding people living in his house?"

"I guess so," Tommy blared. He buzzed the engine and tore

down the driveway backward, narrowly missing Chuck's mailbox down below.

"Do you think he left something in the cabin? Something he needed?" Lola asked.

Tommy cranked the truck into another gear and then shot from reverse to forwards, pointing the nose of the truck toward the taillights of Chuck's.

"I imagine so. Who knows? He might have had some cash stowed away in the walls or something," Tommy affirmed. "I've met guys who did the same elsewhere. But on Martha's Vineyard? Gosh. Bad people really do pop up everywhere. Thanking my lucky stars, you were with me tonight when it happened."

"Why?" Lola asked, breathless.

"Because he's going to do his best to get rid of me on this wild goose chase, and I have a feeling you know the Vineyard like the back of your hand," Tommy said with a cheeky grin.

Lola cracked her knuckles as Tommy smashed his foot harder against the gas. When they reached the end of the dirt road, Chuck turned right on Edgartown Vineyard Haven Road and chugged south and east, past the Island Alpaca Company. Tommy's foot had no interest in giving up the gas pedal. His eyes meant business.

They shot toward the Manuel F. Correllus State Forest, where Chuck made a frantic right turn onto Barnes Road and chugged south.

"He thought he would lose us there," Tommy said, gripping the steering wheel with white knuckles. "He was wrong."

"Stay alert, because there are several ways he could lose us through here," Lola said. "It's all state forest around here, winding and curving roads, and—oh! Look! He turned left!"

Tommy yanked after him onto Sanderson Ave, then jerked immediately left again when Chuck went north on the same road. Lola clung to her seatbelt, as though that would keep her in one piece, and watched the trees as they whipped by in the grey darkness outside. When they reached Fire Road, Chuck burned right, and Tommy drove right on after him, never allowing him out of sight for long.

"Where do you think he wants to go?" Lola demanded.

"Too late for the ferries tonight now," Tommy affirmed. "I imagine he has a boat docked somewhere on the island. Maybe he's been sleeping there, biding his time."

The race continued. Lola prayed that somehow, some way, a cop would notice them and decide to pull Chuck over. Unfortunately, now that tourist season had begun to trickle to a close, she knew the cops had begun to ease up, take a much-deserved break from the chaos. She had a feeling more than a few of them were crowded around a high-top at the Edgartown Bar, celebrating the end of summer.

"The island feels insanely small when you drive it at this speed," Tommy said with a dry laugh.

Although Chuck seemed to try to go around eighty-five, ninety miles per hour, it was obvious that he just couldn't, not without driving off the road. Just before he barreled into Edgartown, he swept south again, then courted Tommy and Lola around a few little side roads before heading west again.

"He can't shake us," Tommy grumbled. "What does he think he's going to do? Teleport out of here?"

As they continued to chase Chuck, Lola texted Susan, Scott, and Christine with news of what they'd seen.

LOLA: Chuck Frampton is on the island. We're chasing him in a car. Call the police? We're heading west on West Tisbury Road.

CHRISTINE: What? How did you find him?

LOLA: He just rolled into his old cabin like he owned the place (ha).

SCOTT: Calling the cops now. Hold him as long as you can.

SCOTT: He used to dock a boat in Chilmark.

SCOTT: He might be headed that way.

SCOTT: AH!

Lola chuckled and turned her eyes back toward the dark road. "Scott is freaking out."

"I should say," Tommy said. "To be honest, I'm freaking out, too. I don't know how much more of this I can take. My anxiety is through the roof."

"I watched you handle that storm like it was a light rain. This is only Chuck Frampton we're talking about. He's the equivalent of a rat. He doesn't deserve your anxiety," Lola returned.

Scott texted for more details about where they were headed so that he could inform the police. Not long after they entered West Tisbury, sirens blared behind them. Chuck cut north and then rounded west again, down North Road, until he managed to find a road that cranked out toward the Nantucket Sound. The sirens seemed to bounce off of every tree stump and howl into the enormous black sky.

"I don't know why he doesn't just stop!" Lola cried, growing frantic with all the noise. "What does he think he's going to do? Drive the car into the water?"

"I wouldn't put it past him to be so delusional," Tommy affirmed.

As they neared the water, Lola gripped the handle on the door, clinging to it for dear life. She wondered what the hell ran through Chuck's mind at this moment. Someone had been at his house; someone had taken over his land. Surely, wherever he'd kept the money, it was stored somewhere in the belly of that place—and he was hungry for it.

"What kind of low-life scum do you have to be to take advantage of your family and friends like that?" Tommy grumbled.

When the road opened up a bit more, the police officers cranked around Lola and Tommy and barreled toward Chuck. Eventually, they cornered him at the road that overlooked the water. Chuck's truck shot sideways and looked as though it was about to teeter off the edge and into the waves. Lola gasped and clutched her cheeks.

The cop who had driven and the cop in the passenger seat of the lead vehicle crept out of the car, both with their guns drawn. It looked directly out of a scene in a movie. As they surrounded Chuck, Lola and Tommy got out of their truck slowly, as well, totally captivated.

"Chuck, we need you to get out of the truck with your hands over your head," the officer yelled out.

If Lola's memory served her, the officer who had just spoken was one she'd gone to high school with. This meant that he had probably known Chuck his entire life.

How the tables turned.

With a last-second ditch in-mind, Chuck cranked to the side of the truck and tried to drop out the passenger side. Unfortunately for him, another officer raced around that side and latched him tightly, pulling his arms behind his back.

"Chuck, this is going to be a lot easier for you if you don't struggle," the officer blared.

"Those people. They were on my property!" Chuck cried. "I just wanted to go home."

"Don't play dumb, Chuck. You left the island months ago because you're wanted in an investigation relating to several hundred thousands of dollars stolen off the island," the officer said.

"I don't know anything about that," Chuck said.

"Then we'll take you into the station and explain more!" the officer said, feigning cheerfulness.

He dragged Chuck back toward the police car. Lola and Tommy looked just beyond. To Lola's intense dissatisfaction, his eyes connected with hers almost immediately.

"Lola Sheridan," he said. "Good to see you again! You were always the best of the Sheridan sisters."

Lola strung her arms across her chest and glared at him.

"You'll tell them that I didn't have anything to do with this, won't you?" Chuck blared. "You'll tell them that I just wanted to come back to visit my family? Scott sold Frampton Freight, without even consulting me! Can you believe that?"

"Shut up, Chuck. You're going to get what you deserve," Lola returned.

Chuck stuttered. "Lola, come on. After all, we've been through?"

"And what's that been, Chuck?"

"You know. Scott and Susan. We're practically family. We..."

"There's a funny thing about family. Maybe you haven't learned it yet," Lola retorted. She stepped closer to him. She felt light as air, apt to float off the ground with rage. "Family doesn't steal thousands and thousands of dollars from family." She shrugged. "I don't know. Just something to think about for next time. That is if there is a next time."

Chuck cried out some curse words as he was shoved into the back-end of the police car. Lola shook angrily as Tommy swung a thick arm over her and held her close against him. He whispered in her ear, "It's going to be okay. We got him."

One of the officers approached, adjusting his hat so that his ears wiggled up and down.

"We're going to need to ask you guys some questions," he told them. "Do you mind stopping by at the station this evening? I know it's late."

Tommy looked at Lola. "You good?"

"Yes! Not a problem," Lola said. "Whatever you need, officer."

CHAPTER 20

Neither Tommy nor Lola could think of much to say as they snaked their way back, slower this time, toward Oak Bluffs. After a strange silence, Lola dialed Scott's number and held her phone to her ear.

"Lola, hey. What's up? What's happened?"

Scott sounded totally frantic, which was understandable considering the situation.

"They got him," Lola breathed. "We're headed to the station right now. Want to meet us there?"

"Yes. I'll get in the car now," Scott affirmed.

Lola hung up and snuck her phone back in her bag. She gave Tommy a glance, only to realize that he actually wore a slight smile. She turned her head totally toward him and said, "What has you so happy, Tommy Gasbarro?"

Tommy laughed. "I don't know. I haven't had a high-speed

chase in a few years. It's thrilling. Always makes me feel like Indiana Jones."

"In a few years?" Lola demanded. "You've done something like that before?"

"Not in the States," Tommy answered. "This was over in Poland after this guy stole my wallet. We had just been sailing in the Baltic Sea and had a few too many beers in a port bar. Next thing I knew, I had borrowed the bartender's car and shot down the road to trap this guy down."

"Did you manage to get him?" Lola asked.

"Not in the least," Tommy said with a laugh. "He knew the roads much better than I did. It was after midnight, and he shot out through a few alleys and I never saw that wallet again. Still, it was almost worth it. Like I told you before, I love the chase."

Lola grinned madly. She reached over and squeezed Tommy's hand over the gearshift. Her heart fluttered. Before she had known what she'd done, she dropped her hand again and pointed. "Look. The precinct is right there. And Scott's already arrived."

As Lola and Tommy parked, Scott and Susan hopped out of Scott's truck. Susan's red hair caught the soft light of the moon, and she wore a trendy leather jacket that Lola had never seen before. She cut toward Lola and wrapped her in a big-sister, little-sister hug and whispered, "I can't believe this happened! Maybe if I hadn't been so bogged down with everything, I might have noticed he was on his way back. Maybe I..."

"Not everything has to be on your shoulders, Susie," Lola said. "Besides. Tommy and I tracked him down."

"What a relief," Susan said. She then bent toward Lola's ear to whisper, "Just between us, but Scott is a literal basket case. I can't calm him down."

"I guess that's to be expected," Lola said, stealing a glance at Scott.

"He's really grown to hate Chuck."

"I can't understand why? He seems so cheerful," Lola said, laughing. "Definitely someone I want to have around at Christmas."

Susan, Lola, and Tommy followed Scott as he burst into the precinct. One of the officers who had been at the scene, who wore a nametag that said, "Will," nodded to all of them.

"The Sheridan Clan," he said. "Scott. Thanks for coming in so late."

"You've got him back there?" Scott demanded.

"Yes. He's in a cell, awaiting questioning," the man said. "He wants to request a lawyer."

Scott arched his brow toward Susan, who just shook her head. "I don't think Chuck Frampton wants me to represent him. We're not exactly on the same side."

The four of them were taken into a side room for a first-round of questioning. Lola and Tommy explained what had happened at Chuck's house, that he'd probably come back for a reason associated with money or his ultimate get-away.

"I think we'd better do a big sweep of his place again, just to see what he was looking for," Will the officer said, marking something in his notes.

"Yes, but, if possible, not for the next few days," Tommy interjected.

Of course, Lola thought. Stan was back at the house, sleeping off his surgery. Tommy didn't want to move him.

Despite the fact that she supposedly hated Stan Ellis more than any other creature on earth, this act of generosity and love warmed her heart.

After another few questions, Lola, Tommy, Scott, and Susan were shown the door of the little questioning room. Back in the hallway, Scott spun on one heel and said, "I would really like to speak to him once tonight, if possible. I haven't seen him since I accused him of what he had done. My mind has flipped around so many times since then. The brother I thought I'd had..."

Will extended a hand and gave a firm nod. "Of course. He's just down here."

Susan, Lola, and Tommy remained far back in the hallway, their gaze cut toward Scott as he marched toward the final doorway.

"He's handcuffed to the table, waiting for another line of questioning," Will informed Scott. "So when I open the door, he won't be able to get up. He won't be able to do anything."

"Okay," Scott said. His apprehension was palpable.

Will opened the door with a squeak. Scott hovered outside the door without speaking for a long time. Finally, he placed his hands on his hips. His lower lip seemed to jump around, as though he was on the verge of tears. Lola knew he would never allow his volatile older brother to see him cry.

"Chuck," Scott said.

"Scott." The voice grumbled out of the room.

"I see you made it back to the Vineyard."

"You know that a Vineyard guy can't stay away for long," Chuck returned angrily.

Scott coughed. Lola clutched Tommy's arm with tight fingers. What could two brothers who'd never had much in common, who'd never been honest with one another—who'd never had anything but time and the freight business to keep them together—say to one another now, after so much had happened?

"I need you to know that I won't fight for you," Scott blared. "You stole from the family who's taken me in. The Sheridans have given me everything. The others you stole from, they were our friends, our relatives. How could you do something like that, Chuck? How could you feast off the backs of others?"

"Listen to yourself, Scott. It's just like you always were before. You're soft. You're pathetic. If you had any sort of..."

"I'm not the one locked to that table, Chuck," Scott blared. He coughed and turned his eyes toward the ground. "When it comes time for it, I will testify against you. The people of the Vineyard deserve all reparations. And I never want to see you again."

"Then get the hell out of here!" Chuck cried. "I hate looking at your nasty face."

Scott turned on his heel. His hands clenched at his sides and he glared forward, a strange mix of enraged and stoic. When he reached them, he nodded and said, "I just wanted to know what it would feel like to see him one last time."

"What did it feel like?" Susan asked. She snaked her fingers through his.

"It felt like nothing," Scott said with a shrug. "It felt like looking at a stranger."

CHAPTER 21

LOLA AND TOMMY RETURNED TO TOMMY'S RENTAL. THEY LED the way back to the main house, which glowed warmly, its many lights lit up to draw them home. As Lola crept from the passenger seat, the back door ripped open to reveal Christine and Audrey, whose eyes were as big as saucers. Audrey rushed down the steps and wrapped her mother in an enormous hug.

"I was so worried!" she cried. She drew back and stuttered for a moment. "You were in a high-speed car chase. We heard about it on the news. What the heck, Mom?"

Tommy rounded the front of the truck. "She was instrumental in the high-speed chase, in fact," he told Audrey. "She knows these roads much better than I ever could. We would have lost him. He might have slipped off the scent, gotten into his boat, and sailed away in the darkness."

Audrey blinked up at Tommy, clearly surprised to see him. Lola realized the two of them had never met—not even at the party after their big sail since Tommy had mostly spent time with the men in the family. She swallowed a lump in her throat and swept an arm over Audrey's shoulders.

"Tommy, this is my daughter, Audrey. Audrey, this is Tommy Gasbarro," she said. She couldn't figure out why, but saying their names together felt like music across her tongue.

"Good to meet you," Tommy said.

"You too," Audrey affirmed. Her eyes sparkled beautifully.

Scott and Susan bounded out of their truck, as well. Scott still looked a bit frantic. Christine beckoned for them all to enter the house, to sit, to relax. When they entered, they found both Wes and Zach inside, still dressed (or dressed again), as though it was going to be a long night and they were fully prepared for the ride.

The air outside had shifted. It was no longer a balmy summer evening; it held the crisp, almost sharp end of near-fall. For the first time in all the months since they had arrived, Christine shut the large door closed, rather than only the screen door. A card table was brought out from the closet, and the puzzle table was cleared to allow more space for sitting, for conversation, and gathering together. Christine popped open a bottle of wine, and Lola popped open another. Audrey went through the pantry and dragged out as many snacks as she could find.

Together, Lola and Tommy did what they could to unpack the events of the evening. It had been a frantic few hours. As they explained the high-speed chase in more detail, Wes looked completely captivated, his eyes searching his youngest daughter's face as though she was a stranger he had just discovered.

"How fascinating," Christine marveled.

"And that's it, then," Susan said. "We've got the guy. Chuck

Frampton is now behind bars. And since we have such a paper trail behind him, I don't know how he'll get out. Not any time soon, anyway."

The conversation shifted as more wine was poured. Audrey settled into a cross-legged position against the wall with a full bag of potato chips across her admittedly growing stomach, chomping happily. Christine held Zach's hand over the table as she talked about another high-speed chase she had seen when she'd been a Brooklyn nobody back in her twenties. Lola laughed and said, although it was really a good story, she wasn't looking to make a daily habit of something like that.

"Suit yourself," Tommy said. "I'm headed out now to go chase down another bad guy."

"Oh, cool. A hero," Lola said, chuckling.

"It's what this island needs," Tommy joked, winking.

Lola was mesmerized with how easily Tommy stitched himself into the backdrop of her family. Throughout the evening, he took several side-bars with Scott and Zach, before returning with some kind of witty comment about whatever Susan, Christine, Audrey, and Lola spoke of. Lola crept closer to him on the couch they shared, her shoulder heavy against his bicep. Sometimes, he made her laugh so much that her body made the cushions quake.

Just past one in the morning, Christine suggested that Tommy stay on with them that night.

"I'll stay home from the bakery tomorrow and make everyone breakfast," she announced. "I absolutely insist on it."

Tommy's face grew shadowed. He cast his eyes toward Lola's, then returned them to Christine. "I actually have to get back to my place. Er—Chuck's place. Whatever it is."

"It's your place," Scott corrected. "For now and for however long you want or need it."

"Are you sure I can't tempt you with croissants? Eggs? Bacon?" Christine asked.

"Naw. I have to run back," Tommy said. "But I'll take you up on that offer another time, Christine. I promise you that. There's not a lot that I like in this world more than a decent breakfast."

Tommy rose and pulled his keys from his pocket. Lola leaped up and said, "I'll walk you out!" They shot out of the back door and then closed it tightly behind them. Again, Lola was struck with the bizarreness of the house closed-off. Normally, you could hear almost everything from every room, since the screen doors were only invisible buffers.

"Thank you for your help tonight," Lola whispered. Her heart pounded as she gazed into his eyes, totally lost in her desire for him.

"I'm glad you were there. I'm always a little bit glad you're there," Tommy said. He palmed the back of his neck, clearly shocked that he had mustered so much emotion in a single sentence.

"Um." Lola stared at the truck.

Just say it, Lorraine. You're used to getting everything you want, any time you want. Why can't you just get this? This final, fantastic thing?

"You don't want a little more company, do you?"

Finally, she'd added them: the words, the hope, to the universe.

Tommy arched his brow and pondered the question for a moment. "You know who else is at my house, don't you?"

Lola nodded. "I do."

"And you're okay that he's there?"

Lola shrugged and flapped her arms on either side of her thin frame. "I don't know. I only know that I want to be with you. I can figure out a way to deal with the rest."

"Honesty. It's never the best thing to hear, is it?" Tommy said with an ironic laugh.

"I promise you that I'll do my best, to be honest at every turn. No matter how painful it is," Lola murmured.

Suddenly, there before her house, in the glossy sheen of the moonlight, Tommy bent down and kissed her for the first time. It was the kind of kiss that punched her in the back of the knees, the kind of kiss that made her thoughts inarticulate and her arms feel fuzzy. It was a kiss of feeling, of promise, of the future. And when she brought her head back again and blinked back into his face, she had no more words to say except, "Take me home with you."

Tommy couldn't do anything else but agree.

CHAPTER 22

Lola had woken up in the arms of many, many men over the years—but she had never woken up like this.

How could she describe the difference?

Tommy's strong arms spooned her from behind. Through her back, she could feel the rise and fall of his chest as he inhaled, exhaled, still deep in slumber. His musk wrapped around her, thrilling her, and, unconsciously, one of his hands slipped over hers and clung to it—as though, even in dreams, he didn't want to let her go.

Sunlight drifted in through the living room window, carrying with it a gorgeous green glow since trees surrounded them in all directions. She felt as though they lived in a secret clubhouse, a treehouse with their own rules, their own language.

As much as it killed Lola to do it, she eventually slipped out from the sturdy arms of her love, dressed, and headed to the kitchen. Once there, she brewed a pot of coffee and stared at that still-shut door. The coffee maker popped and bubbled, and all the while, that door seemed akin to the Great Wall of China—something totally impenetrable. When it opened, Lola had zero idea of what would happen next. If Stan's seeing them at the hospital in early August was any indication, it wouldn't go well.

Lola had never been Susan or Anna—the kind of woman who oversaw a whole family and prepared big, bountiful breakfasts and ensured everyone got everywhere on time, that sort of thing. Now, with Tommy asleep in one room and Stan Ellis in another, Lola felt this strange urgency. She searched through the fridge and came up with eight eggs, some bacon. The pantry produced sugar and flour, enough ingredients to make pancakes, and it seemed someone—Chuck or Tommy—had even purchased a little thing of maple syrup.

It was like Christine always said. Food brought people together—even people who wouldn't have been paired together in the first place. It was sustenance; it was nourishing; it was something to talk about; it forced you to look someone in the eye and engage with them in ways that, in other instances, wasn't possible.

Sure, it was just a simple breakfast. But it was breakfast prepared for two men who hadn't ever really had anyone but one another and, most important of all, Anna Sheridan.

Anna Sheridan had been their guiding light in the darkness.

And then one day, she'd been gone.

She'd never come back.

And Lola was borderline tired of the endless charade of blame.

Maybe Stan had already paid for what he had done. He'd given himself a kind of life-sentence, a world of solitude, time and time after time, all entrenched in his own horror and guilt.

Lola splayed the fried eggs and bacon on a large blue platter and placed it at the center of the breakfast table. She then poured all coffees, a bit of orange juice, and dotted each and every pancake in a beautiful tower on another orange plate. She blinked down at what she had created—reminiscent of something you might see on TV—and felt totally pleased with herself. Now, all she had to do was wait.

And she didn't have to wait long.

The door between herself and Stan Ellis creaked open only a minute or two later. Stan appeared in the crack, stooped-over, exhausted, with enormous bags beneath his eyes. His grizzled hair created a halo around his skull, and he looked like he'd lost maybe ten or fifteen pounds from his already thin frame—presumably because of his health problems.

He blinked down at Lola from that crack in the door. Utter shock played over his face. Finally, after a long pause, he said, "Are you trying to kill me?"

Lola, who remained seated at the breakfast table with her hands folded beneath her chin, just shook her head.

Stan placed his elbow on the edge of the doorframe and leaned heavily against his hand. For the next minute or two, they regarded one another. Lola couldn't help but try to imagine what this man might have become if her mother had actually left Wes for him. Would they have lived a long and happy life together? Would she have loved the wild hair, the big eyes, the cheekbones? Would they have laughed?

And what would she have looked like beside him?

"You know you look exactly like her, don't you?" Stan said suddenly.

The words were like a knife through the heart. It was one thing to hear them constantly from her sisters, from her father, from others on the Vineyard. It was another to hear the words from her mother's lover himself.

"I just turned thirty-nine," Lola returned. "A year older than she ever was."

Stan dropped his eyes toward the breakfast. He looked exhausted, even more so than he had minutes before. This hadn't been Lola's hope. She swept her fingers through her hair and gestured.

"Please, sit. I heard you had surgery. I only wanted to help," she said.

Stan crept toward the chair across from her and sat slowly. He blinked down at the eggs, the bacon, and said, "It looks better than anything I've had in years, Lola. Is it okay to call you that?"

She nodded and gave him a small smile. Lola was frankly surprised that he had known which one of the Sheridan sisters she was. Of course, she also had to imagine that Stan knew a great deal more about her and her sisters than she wanted to give him credit for. The pictures of them in his head were probably twenty-some years old, sure—but not so much had changed, personality-wise.

Lola helped Stan pile up his breakfast plate, grateful to have something to do with her hands. When she sat back down, she realized her hands were shaking from the sheer anxiety of the awkward situation.

Lola had thought maybe, given this time alone with Stan; she might want to pepper him with questions about her mother. She thought she might demand answers about that night: why the hell had he turned off the lights, or why he'd lived and the others hadn't! Why!

But instead, she hung in the silence, marveling at the time and space the two of them had had to live without her.

That moment, Tommy appeared in the doorway between the kitchen and the living area, where she and Tommy had slept. He scrubbed at his dark curls and nodded toward Stan, clearly confused.

"You made breakfast?"

"Sure did," Lola affirmed. "Sit down. Eat with us."

"We were worried you'd never get up," Stan said. "Lazybones."

"Hey!" Tommy said.

Lola laughed so hard that her stomach shook. She placed a napkin over her lips and watched as Tommy and Stan shared a furtive look. If she had read it properly, it had said something like: *I don't know why she's here, why she isn't mad, why this is working. But just go along with it, okay?*

Tommy informed Stan about the events of the previous evening: the wild car chase, the arrest of Chuck Frampton. Stan's eyes bulged out in shock.

"You're telling me that while I slept in that little room, a real-live criminal tried to break in here?" he asked.

"I guess technically it is his place," Tommy said, shrugging.

"Still! And then, you just went off after him! Like that!" Stan snapped his fingers like a cartoon character.

Lola hadn't envisioned him to be so peppy, so whimsical. She imagined her mother's laugh ringing out from the bed they'd surely shared back at his little cabin. She imagined her mother's heart feeling free in ways it never could have with Wes Sheridan.

"I only met Chuck a handful of times," Stan said. "A few times at the bar down in Edgartown. He was never a very polite guy. I saw him berate Rita, the bartender. She didn't take a liking to that. Last I heard, he wasn't allowed back."

"I guess he's not technically allowed anywhere right now," Lola said.

"It's just a sad thing when people on this island turn on one another," Stan said. "I'm not a Vineyard-born like you. I came when I was thirty. But back then, I was captivated by the level of camaraderie on the island. It felt as though, no matter who someone was or what they thought about you, they would go out of their way to help. It got addicting, really. By the time I thought it might have been appropriate for me to leave, I couldn't think of another single place on the planet to go. Not like you, girls. You all had such promise. So much to give the world. And you went out and you got what you needed. Now? Do you plan to stay?"

Lola's lips parted. She glanced back toward Tommy, whose dark ones burned back. There was so much she didn't know about whatever had just happened between them; there was so much she wanted to demand of Tommy—in the style of, *can we be together? Can we be all I've ever really dreamed of? Are you actually the one I've been looking for all this time?*

"I get it. It's too much of a personal question," Stan admitted. "And it's never good to have such serious discussions at the breakfast table."

Stan grabbed his knife and lifted the butter. As he tried to scrape the knife over the creamy yellow, his hand began to quake so violently that he actually had to put the butter container down. He balked at himself, then tried to make a joke.

"I guess it's time to put new batteries in these hands," he said.

"That's all right, Dad. I got it," Tommy said.

Tommy grabbed the butter container and the knife and began to smear across the toast, whistling as he did it. Lola was completely overwhelmed with this act of generosity. Number one: Tommy had called Stan "Dad," which totally blew her over. But number two: she'd never envisioned Tommy Gasbarro to be the kind of guy to pause to help someone put butter on their toast.

It was a morning of impossibilities. This was how she would think about it in the future. The conversation popped and fluttered; she laughed outrageously at both Stan and Tommy's jokes, especially when they tried to one-up each other. She brewed another pot of coffee for all of them and stewed in her own full-feeling, a wide smile stretched between her cheeks.

Slowly, Stan rose from the breakfast table and hobbled back toward the bedroom. At the doorframe, he paused again and turned back.

"Thank you for breakfast, Lola," he said.

"You're very welcome, Stan."

"I know there's still a lot to say," Stan declared. "Stuff I can't go over at this moment, since I can barely get my mind straight. But I want to invite you and Christine and Susan over to my house soon when I'm well enough to cook. Do you think you could convince them to come along with you?"

Lola nodded and gave him a soft, genuine smile. "I will certainly try."

"Good," Stan said. "I can't believe I'm saying this, but I've waited for this for a very long time."

When the door clicked closed between them, Lola placed her hands over her eyes and burst into tears. Her father had always said she was the crier of the family, and here she was, at it again. Tommy, now accustomed to her quick shifts in mood, placed a hand on her shoulder and guided her body into his. She placed her cheek against his chest and shuddered, her tears both happy and sad, the most confusing of all.

"Come on. Let's go outside," Tommy murmured.

"We have to clean up."

"I'll do that later," Tommy said. "Grab your jacket."

It was the tail-end of the first week of September. Lola pulled her jacket on and stepped into the early light of the morning. All the skin on the back of her neck tightened with a chill. Tommy guided her toward the line of trees and leaned her heavily against one of the trunks and drew a line down her cheek with his finger. His gaze was powerful, an affirmation of his growing affection for her.

"I wanted to kiss you every day on that sailboat trip," he told her.

"Why didn't you?" Lola murmured.

"I was afraid of what would happen, I guess," Tommy said. "And I worried about our connection to Stan. I worried that you could never forgive him for what he did. And know that I don't take it lightly."

"I know you don't," Lola said.

"Good," he said.

To clear their heads, Lola and Tommy walked through the woods quietly together. Early-autumn birds flickered through the tip-tops of the trees; some of the leaves had begun to anticipate the later months, lining themselves with red and orange. Lola and Tommy fell into an easy rhythm with one another. Surprisingly, they spoke very little about the car chase or about Stan, and instead focused on one another, the important things they wanted to reveal to one another as middle-aged people, on the verge of some kind of love story.

Slowly, they made their way back toward the water. Once there, Tommy lifted a perfect, flat stone from the sand and skipped it over the water.

"Three times? Not bad," Lola said. She collected her own stone and cast it out—skipping it no fewer than five times.

Tommy whistled. "I should have known that I couldn't compete with an island girl."

"That's right. We were born with magic in our fingers," Lola replied with a slight grin.

Later that morning, Lola said, "I don't know how I'm going to convince Christine and Susan to go to Stan's house. It took a lot of pulling for Susan to get Christine and I to return to the island in the first place. Seriously, I almost didn't come."

"Really? What were you so busy with?"

"My life in Boston. Partying, since Audrey had been away and I had this whole other life. Trying to figure out who I was, now that she's gone. That kind of thing," Lola said. "When I came out after Susan's request, I told myself it would only be a few weeks. But something about that first month sparked a fire in me. I was back almost instantly after I had left. The same was true for Christine."

"It's intoxicating," Tommy agreed.

"But we've all done a lot of forgiving this summer," Lola continued. "We had to find a way to forgive our father, for one. And we had to forgive one another, after so many years apart. I don't know if forgiving Stan is in the cards for us. It might be a single step too far. Of course, there's no reason we shouldn't try."

CHAPTER 23

LOLA AND TOMMY PARTED WAYS THAT EARLY-AFTERNOON. Lola admitted she had to send a few follow-up emails for potential clients, and Tommy both wanted to check on Stan and head to his boat for a few hours, to clear his head. At this, Lola's mind raced. Did he want to clear his head of her? Of what they had done? Of what they were maybe on the verge of becoming? But in the strange silence, Tommy gripped her hand and said, "It's just my form of meditation. That's all."

This calmed her immediately: both the fact that he wanted this and the fact that it seemed like he could actually read her mind enough to ease it.

Lola took the car she'd left at Chuck's place back to the main house. She had that once familiar feeling about her—as though she had just spent a whole night partying and was now strung-out, exhausted, yet thrilled with the memories. Naturally, she was no longer that wild, maniac partier.

This was better, anyway.

It was warmer by this time of the day, and the thick door between the porch that overlooked the Sound and the inside living area had been opened once more. Christine, Audrey, and Susan's voices chirped like birds. Lola crept toward the sound, listening, not wanting them to know she was there yet.

"I never imagined her to be a vintage wedding dress person," Susan stated. "But she said she stumbled into this boutique she says she needs to show me when I come back to Newark. You can tell she's ready to pick a dress. All this waiting is killing her."

"Whatever, Aunt Susie. All she wants is for you to get better," Audrey said. "She would wear a tarp over her body if it meant you were there beside her."

"That's right. When Amanda broke the news to Richard that I would walk her down the aisle instead of him, he apparently didn't take it so well," Susan said. "Poor guy."

"Poor guy? I won't hear of that," Lola interjected, bolting out onto the porch and beaming at her sisters and daughter.

Just as Audrey had done with Christine, she now play-acted as though she couldn't believe how late in the day it already was or how scandalous it was that Lola had slept over at a man's place.

"We were worried, sick!" Audrey cried. "You went out to say goodbye to him and then? It was like he kidnapped you out of thin air. Nowhere to be found. I was sick over it."

"I think you might have been sick over those potato chips you inhaled last night. Not me going home with a guy," Lola said.

Christine grinned. She hustled toward the picnic table and poured Lola a glass of wine and then gestured for her to join them. "Tell us everything. We're dying here."

"Ha." Lola accepted the glass and then sat on the floor in front of her sisters and Audrey, as though they were the grand committee and she had come to get their approval. "All I can say is... I'm falling for him. Hard."

"My gosh," Susan said. She splayed her hand over her heart and beamed. "I never thought you would try to settle down again. Not after Timothy."

"Timothy is about half the man that Tommy is," Lola clarified.

"Hey! That's my father you're talking about," Audrey said playfully, before inhaling the rest of her orange juice and smacking her lips.

"Right. I know how you treasure his memory," Lola said with a laugh.

"He looks at you like you're the first woman he's ever seen," Christine said. "He's amazed by you."

"I always thought he was a huge introvert, but you could tell he loved being with our family last night," Susan said.

Lola tipped her wine glass ever-so-slightly and considered this, how to approach the topic at hand.

"That's not really the only thing I have to tell you about, though," Lola said, not making eye contact with her sisters just yet.

"Ah! Now it gets explicit," Audrey joked.

"No! Audrey. Gosh. No. Okay, so. The reason Tommy had to go back to Chuck's last night is that he's in the middle of caring for Stan. He had minor surgery, and Tommy is watching over him until he can stay by himself again," Lola finally said. She stole a quick glance at each of her sisters.

Immediately, the mood on the porch shifted completely. It was like the clouds had formed overhead. Christine, in particular, looked stormy.

"You must have avoided him, right?" she asked, crossing her arms over her chest. "Was he asleep the whole time?"

Lola fumbled over her words. "He woke up this morning. And I cooked him breakfast. And then we talked for a bit."

Susan stood slowly from the porch swing. She placed her hand on her stomach and stepped out toward the railing, gazing out across the water. Nobody spoke for a long time.

"Wow. Stan Ellis," Susan marveled finally.

Lola couldn't read the tone in her voice. Was it volatile, on the verge of an explosion? Was it disappointment, as though Lola had taken everything three stages too far?

Christine shifted and sipped her wine. Everyone's eyes seemed to gaze into an impossible distance, despite them all sitting on the same porch.

Finally, Christine said, "What did he seem like?"

Lola bit down on her lower lip. How could she say this without giving a disservice to her dad, to the accident, to any of it?

"He seemed lovely," Lola whispered. "I hate to say this, but. I understood. Not all of it—no way could I ever fully comprehend what Mom did or how it all ended, but I understood why she wanted to be with him."

"Huh." Susan lifted her hand to her wig, as though she wanted to check to make sure it was still there.

"I don't know how we'll find a way through this," Lola said. "The only thing I know for sure is this. We've all made countless mistakes. Mom's mistakes still lurk amongst us, even though she's been dead since 1993."

"My mistake still has about six months to germinate," Audrey interjected.

"Thank you, Audrey," Lola said. "Stan wants to have the three of us over for dinner when he's well enough. I know it might be a difficult thing to grapple with. But would you please think about it? If not for him, then for me and for Tommy. I think this really is my next love. Maybe the forever one, this time."

They were silent again for a long time. Suddenly, there was a torrential downpour of footsteps from the upstairs to the downstairs. The screen door erupted to reveal a youthful-looking Wes, a bucket hat on his head and binoculars flapping at his chest.

"Who's ready to go?" he called.

Apparently, the girls had given a half-hearted "yes" to the call of bird-watching in the boat along the edge of the Vineyard. Christine grabbed a bottle of white from the fridge and stabbed her feet into her flip flops. Her eyes finally met with Lola's, and she gave a slight shrug.

"Just let me think about it, okay? It's a huge request and I'm not sure that I'm ready just yet."

"You're the one who wanted to accost him a few months ago," Lola said.

"Yeah? Well. Now, I'm in love, and I have the best job I've ever had, and I'm going to be a stand-in mother," Christine said, her voice hushed so that Wes didn't hear. "I don't have to yell at Stan Ellis at a bar anymore."

"Then let's just have dinner with him. Please," Lola said under her breath. "I swear this is the last thing I'll ask you to do."

Down at the boat, Wes spoke excitedly about the birds he wanted to point out to Audrey, while Lola unhooked the rope.

Christine sat at the steering wheel and cranked the engine, while Audrey opened another bag of chips. As she ate, she carefully put a slice of avocado on each and gestured to Lola.

"Look. I'm thinking about what you told me. Nutrients."

"Very good," Lola said absently. "I know your baby will thank you later on in life."

"If she's anything like me, she'll be like—what are these nutrients? Why aren't we eating chips exclusively?" Audrey returned. "Ah, but actually, Amanda has me going on a fancy diet with her. Obviously, she wants to be cut for the wedding, and I need to gain. But it's got loads of colors in it. I had no idea they made orange peppers, did you?"

"You're making me look like a really responsible mother," Lola said. "Thanks for that."

Christine eased the boat west and south, along the coast, close enough that Wes could point out the various water birds along the way—the storks and the bank swallow birds. He whipped off his binoculars in a hurry and gave them to Audrey throughout, telling her details about each of the birds. The facts were actually fascinating, and Christine, Susan, and Lola soon took the binoculars for themselves for better inspection.

Christine docked the boat, and the family got out to sit on the sand for a while. Audrey and Wes sat together and spoke with excitement about the birds that were more interesting to spot during winter. Wes promised to show Audrey as many as he could, come wind, snow, or rain. Audrey thanked him and said, "Maybe not as much snow as you're talking about, but I can handle a little wind and rain."

Christine sat beside Lola and stripped off her dress to reveal a two-piece beneath. Lola smirked and said, "New suit? I thought you said you would never wear a two-piece after forty."

Christine shrugged. "Things change. I decided a super-flat belly isn't my number one priority these days. Would you pass those chips?"

"If I can take them from Audrey," Lola said. She lurched forward, grabbed the bag, and placed them between herself and Christine.

"Thank you." Christine tipped her teeth against the edge of the chip and gazed out across the waves. "Zach brought something up with me last night. I guess while you and Tommy were out on your car chase."

"Ha. What was that?"

"He thinks we should consider moving in together by the end of the year," she said. "I've moved in with people quickly before, back in New York, but it was usually because I had nowhere else to stay or couldn't afford my rent."

"What did it feel like when he suggested it?" Susan, who sat on the other side of Christine, asked.

"I was surprised at my mix of feelings," Christine offered. "On the one hand, I was so excited that he wanted to start a life with me in that way. But on the other hand, I have absolutely loved living at our old place. Every day when I return from the bistro, I know one of you rascals is going to be around to chat with, to gossip with. It makes me remember how much I missed you all over the years."

Christine's eyes sparkled with the images, as though she was on the brink of tears. Lola wrapped her arm around her and said, "We're going to be on the island for good. All of us."

Susan nodded. "No matter who ends up in the house, in the

end, we're all welcome there, all the time. It's the heartbeat within all of us."

The three sisters held onto one another after that, huddled close, listening to the waves and the laughter from Wes and Audrey, who had fallen into a level of banter that seemed rare between grandfathers and their granddaughters.

"I don't want the summer to end," Lola whispered.

"I'm afraid it basically already has," Susan said with a laugh.

"School's already started," Christine added.

"And the air is different. You can feel it. The island is ready for something else."

"Autumn."

They said the word as though it was pure poetry. They said it as though it offered them everything they needed. Renewal. Rest. A deep breath after what had been one of the biggest seasons of their lives.

CHAPTER 24

Over the next weeks, Lola's relationship with Tommy found new strength: humor lined with empathy, intelligent conversations with their own zest for life. Mid-September, Tommy helped Stan move back into his little cabin, which meant the time had come for Stan to offer, and offer again, his place for dinner.

It finally happened when Tommy was out on a mid-autumn sailing expedition across the Nantucket Sound. Susan had finished her chemotherapy a week before and had far more energy than normal, a bit more pep to her step. They still waited on tests to learn about the cancer itself, whether it had stuck around in the face of chemo, but their overall feeling was hopeful. The Sheridan sisters had weathered another storm.

Christine was the one to bring up the dinner. It was October first, and they sat hunched around the puzzle table with Audrey, whose stomach had recently performed a little dance and popped out over her jeans—something she seemed to find endlessly funny.

Audrey was stationed over her computer, penning an article for an upcoming issue of the Penn State newspaper. She had even decided to do a few online classes that semester, to ensure she didn't get too behind. In general, she seemed confident, happy, albeit the tiniest bit annoyed that the Sheridan sisters didn't like a lot of quiet. It made it difficult for her to work.

"Are you sure you're ready?" Lola asked.

"Even if I'm not fully ready, I think it's better to face our demons," Christine offered. "I already know what dessert I'm going to make. Even if we have the most miserable time in the world, we'll follow it up with dessert and it will be worth it."

Lola checked with Stan about the following evening. He whole-heartedly agreed.

"I'll come in early from fishing to prepare everything," he told her excitedly over the phone. "Oh, gosh. I guess it's finally time to do some dusting I haven't gotten around to for the past two-odd years."

"Don't worry about it. We're pretty low-maintenance," Lola said with a laugh. "Just feed us, and we'll be happy."

During the hours before the girls left for Stan's, they finished up the last paint job on one of the new bedrooms. They'd decided on ivory in the right bedroom and lilac in the other. They had purchased new bedsheets to match the colors and hung photographs and artwork all over the walls. As they'd painted and decorated, they had played all of their mother's favorites songs—an act that had caused Wes to sing and whistle for hours on end.

"I think it looks great," Lola breathed, analyzing the last of their work from the center of the living room, hands on her hips.

"Now, our kids are going to keep having babies, and we'll have to keep adding on more rooms," Susan said. "And Christine, there's no telling how many babies you'll raise in this world."

"No, telling," Christine affirmed. "But I know they'll know this house. Whoever they are."

Christine drove them toward Stan's house that early evening in October. Her hands clenched the wheel of the car a bit too tightly, and her eyebrows hovered close over her eyes. When she hit a pothole, she yelped.

"Sorry. My anxiety is through the roof," she said. "Everything is affecting me right now."

Rain plopped across the window shield as Christine eased them down a bumpy dirt road, far down to the very end, where Stan's little house lurked over a little dock. His familiar boat was latched to it, bobbing slightly. The water beneath it had already captured the orange and pink of sunset.

Christine had made a lemon meringue pie, one of her specialties, and the girls had brought plenty of wine to share between themselves and Stan. Together, they walked up the little path toward Stan's weathered door.

"Hard to imagine Mom doing this," Susan said.

"I think she wanted adventure," Lola murmured. "I think it makes sense."

Before they could knock, Stan yanked open the door and grinned broadly at them through the screen. Of course, the silence stretched between them, then. He felt awkward about his quick greeting, and he turned his eyes away and mumbled, "Welcome! Thanks for um... Thank you for coming tonight." The screen door screeched as he pressed it open.

"Hey," Lola said. She lifted up to give him a little hug. "I guess you already know who everyone is. This is Christine, and this is Susan."

"Of course," Stan said. He placed his hands on his hips and beheld them. It was obvious that he'd tried his best to tame his grizzled hair; he was recently showered, and he had gained a tiny bit of weight since the last time Lola had seen him. He looked almost handsome, and there was a twinkle to his eyes— the humor Lola had a hunch had attracted their mother in the first place.

"Sit down! Please, sit," he said, gesturing toward the little table, set for four.

"Thank you," Christine said. "We brought wine. Would you like some?"

Christine poured each of them a glass of the Cabernet Sauvignon. Stan fumbled through conversation, making it pretty known that he hadn't had a proper dialogue with anyone who wasn't Tommy or a doctor in the past, maybe ten years. Lola inspected the shelves in his house. He had, in fact, dusted. There was no telling how long it had taken him to deep clean his little house.

"I cooked brisket," he said suddenly. "It's out in the smoker. I just have to get it out of there and slice it off. Do you girls mind if I head out and..."

"Not at all!" Susan piped.

In Lola's mind, she seemed a little too obvious about wanting him to get out of there.

Stan scurried away. The Sheridan sisters analyzed the interior of the little house. From where they sat, they could see the bed, which seemed to dip in the center. Already, Lola and Tommy had formulated which side of the bed belonged to whom. Stan had slept alone for over twenty-five years.

"It's a nice place," Susan said as she looked around the room.

"You don't have to be the one to make everything feel okay," Christine said—snapping in previous Christine fashion. She dropped her eyes and then muttered, "Sorry. I'm a bit panicked."

"Aren't we all?" Susan returned, giving her younger sister a glare.

"Not Lola." Christine shrugged.

Stan reappeared with a large platter of brisket. He laid it at the center of the table and said, "Your mom used to love it when I smoked this. She liked it with this barbecue sauce recipe, which my mother showed me. Here. I made that, too." He grabbed a jar from the fridge and placed it alongside the brisket. He beamed at them awkwardly, like a little kid who just needed someone to tell him that he had done all right.

"It looks delicious," Susan beamed at him.

"Do you have any um. Buns for sandwiches?" Christine asked.

"Oh! Of course." Stan looked as though he had just committed a huge crime. "They're still outside. I'll grab them."

When he disappeared again, Lola whispered, "It's obvious that he doesn't get a lot of visitors. Why can't you give him a break?"

"I am giving him a break!" Susan cried.

"I can tell by your tone of voice that you're pretending to give him a break, but you're going to talk badly about him to Scott later tonight," Lola hissed.

"It's none of your business what I say to Scott later," Susan said, her nostrils flared.

"I'm for sure talking bad about him to Zach later," Christine admitted. "You can generally count on that."

Lola rolled her eyes. They had completely gone off the rails. Stan returned with the hamburger buns and placed them alongside the sauce and the meat and then collapsed into his chair.

"Sorry. I haven't run around like that since the surgery," he said. "My lower back had this disc problem. I've been back up and at it for the past few weeks, but not so quickly."

"You don't need to hurt yourself for us," Lola said. "We're perfectly fine. I told you; you just have to feed us, and we'll be happy."

Stan placed his hands on the tablecloth and heaved a sigh. "I'm really grateful you girls came here tonight. When I first heard you had returned to the island, I wasn't fully sure what to make of it. I knew that you hadn't known what really happened with your mother and me—at least, I was pretty sure, but I felt that Wes would finally want to clear the air with that, especially since you left him for so long." He scrubbed his cheeks and then blinked out. "There is so much wrong with all of this, obviously. But I think one of the things that hurts me the most is that he took the blame, and then he lost all of you for so long. I don't know why he did that. The only thing I can reason is that he wanted you to have this perfect image of your mother. That was his gift to you."

The words flowed out so quickly that Lola struggled to catch them all. Christine drank so much of her wine during this brief sitting that she had to pour herself another glass. Stan allowed his chin to fall toward his chest.

"You all look so much like her. There's a piece of her in all of you. After knowing bits and pieces about your lives, I know that your mother would be so, so proud of you. All she wanted was for you three to find yourselves. She wanted you to find happiness. She wanted you to find the kind of love that didn't make excuses.

"She hated that she had an affair," Stan continued. "She cried about it almost all the time. She couldn't make peace with it. She loved your father and she loved you three so much. But unfortunately or fortunately for me, for that tiny slice of my life— she also loved me, too."

Susan, Lola, and Christine's eyes were now rimmed with tears. Susan held a hand to her mouth as he continued.

"We got reckless with it," Stan continued. "Your mother and I no longer cared what Wes or the rest of the world thought, especially that early summer in '93. She kept telling me she was going to leave him. That we could finally have our shot. And a part of me really believed her. I have these letters..."

He pulled out several pieces of folded-up paper from his pocket and splayed them across the table: proof that this older man had been the object of real, intense, heart-wrenching affection.

Lola reached for one and unfolded it and caught the very first few lines.

Stan,

When you take me in your arms, I know that no matter where I go in this world, I'll hold your love close to me.

"Wow," Lola breathed.

"She was quite a writer," Stan affirmed. "When I read your article about Tommy, I knew you had gotten her talents, as well."

Lola's cheeks burned red. "Did she ever talk about going into writing?"

"She had a lot of ideas about her future," Stan said. His voice broke at this admission. "She talked about how life was long, the longest thing we have and she didn't just want the era she'd had with you girls and with Wes at the Sunrise Cove Inn. She wanted to have the creativity and bravery to make something else."

"We can understand that," Susan whispered. She dotted a finger at the edge of her eye. "We all got to start over. Some of us, several times. And in every starting over, we learned something new."

"Your mother wanted that. She was wise enough to know it was possible," Stan murmured.

Everyone held this information for a long time. Lola swallowed and hung her head, suddenly oblivious to any idea of hunger. She had dragged her sisters into the lion's den of pain and suffering. But what had she thought would happen?

"I'm sorry to come out with it all like this," Stan said. "I'm not used to human interaction. I tend to mess things up, to make things fall apart. I just wanted to make sure I told you three, while I have you here, during this brief evening—that I don't think she actually would have gone through with it."

"With what?" Christine asked.

"With leaving," Stan affirmed. "As much as she had daydreams and had fantasies, her love for you three and her life was strong. We talked about our future, but I always knew it was lined with pain because it was a future we couldn't truly have." He paused, sucking in a deep breath. "I woke up after the accident a few days later. I had always wondered about comas—what it felt like, where it felt like you'd been," he whispered. "But I can't begin to describe how it felt to emerge from that coma and be told that the great and beautiful love of my life, Anna Sheridan, had died. I can't begin to describe what it felt like to learn that it was all my fault."

Stan knelt his head lower and studied his hands for a long time. To Lola, it seemed obvious that he had spent a lot of the day trying to scrub them and clean out his fingernails. Such was the life of a fisherman.

Suddenly, he ambled back up from his chair. As he walked toward another cabinet, he kept his hand on his lower back, indicating where the surgery had been. When he returned, he had a little photograph of himself and Anna Sheridan during what seemed to be the peak of their romance. Susan took the photo first and blinked at it.

"Wow. You both are so beautiful in this photo," she said before closing her mouth with her hand and laughing. "I can't believe I just said that."

"But it's true," Christine said. She took the photo next.

"I look a lot different," Stan affirmed. "Time really caught up to me. Time and loneliness. Together, they tend to make a lethal cocktail."

Lola got the photo next. It was true that Stan was drop-dead handsome in it, standing next to their gorgeous mother with this look in his eyes that made it seem like he had won the world.

"She was my dream," Stan said. "And now, she lives there still. I dream about her at least once a week still. She gives me advice sometimes. But usually, we just laugh. I liked to laugh with her."

The girls held the silence for a long time. Nobody seemed to know what to say next.

Finally, Lola offered, "Thank you for your honesty, Stan."

"Yes. Thank you," Christine said. Her eyes flashed. "I had no idea what it would be like to meet you properly for the first time. But it was better than expected."

Susan grabbed a napkin and swept it over her cheeks, which were lined with tears.

"I have to say, I've never been hungrier in my life," Susan interjected.

"Me too," Christine said.

"Shall we eat? It looks great, Stan," Lola said.

Slowly, the girls loaded up their burger buns with brisket and barbecue sauce and dug in. Susan poured Stan a glass of wine, but he said he would stick to beer, so Susan shrugged it off and drank it for herself. The conversation became fluid, alive, usually dipping into stories Stan told them about their mother, memories they'd shared.

"Your mother actually taught me how to dance," he said suddenly.

"What?" Christine demanded. "Mom only danced in the kitchen a little bit. She didn't have any real skill, or..."

"That's actually not true," Stan affirmed. "Your mother and I would practice salsa dancing right here in this very kitchen. She was fantastic at it. She said she'd taken classes in high school, but that Wes never had time to dance with her anymore."

Christine's jaw dropped. "You know how to salsa?"

"I think I remember most of it," Stan said. "It's been twenty-five years or so."

"I learned a few years ago in Mexico," Christine said. "Would you um. Would you like to give it a go?"

Lola played a traditional salsa song on her phone and joined Susan on the other side of the table, giving Christine and Stan space. Slowly, Christine and Stan stepped into the rhythm, turning their eyes toward their feet to keep time. It didn't take long for them to put everything together. Soon, they laughed as they twirled around the kitchen, their bodies focused and their eyes glowing.

Lola turned her head toward Susan, who looked awestruck. When the song finished, Lola and Susan clapped their hands, and both Christine and Stan bowed.

"Wow! You really did remember it," Christine said.

"A bit more than I'd expected to," Stan said.

"I think I worked up an appetite. Shall I grab dessert?" Christine said.

They stayed long into the night. When they returned to the main house that night, they found Audrey still awake, a literary magazine strewn across her stomach and her feet up on the couch.

"What are you still doing up?" Lola asked, squeezing her daughter's toes as she entered the living room.

"Wanted to make sure you clowns didn't get into any trouble," Audrey answered. "Off on some kind of adventure with my grandmother's old lover? It sounds like the start of a bad horror movie."

"Ha," Lola said.

"How was it, then?" Audrey asked. She snapped her magazine together and studied the three of them, her eyebrows lowering.

"It was much better than I anticipated," Christine offered.

"He's a dear man," Susan affirmed. "But so lonely."

"You think you'll see him again?" Audrey asked.

The Sheridan sisters glanced at one another, considering it.

"People need people," Christine said with finality. "And it seems like Stan Ellis needs us more than ever right now. To be honest, I think we need him, too."

CHAPTER 25

A WEEK AFTER THE DINNER WITH STAN, LOLA AWOKE AT Tommy's little cabin in the woods—one they had begun to completely redecorate, out with the Chuck and in with the Lola and Tommy. Lola hadn't yet moved in, of course, but she spent enough time there, falling into that haziness of love with her sailor Tommy Gasbarro, that naturally, her flair for design and personality was everywhere. Tommy had begun paying rent to Scott and had even floated the idea of purchasing the place outright. This both thrilled and frightened Lola. After all: she had to question if Tommy truly wanted this life of romantic bliss, of the same-place, no-questions-asked. Already, he had asked her if she wanted to go on another sailing expedition over the winter in the southern hemisphere. Lola had said yes so quickly, she had nearly cut him off.

Yes. I want to go everywhere with you. I want to go everywhere and nowhere. I just want to be in your arms.

Lola dressed quickly and kissed Tommy on the cheek. "I promised I'd be home to watch Dad today," she said.

"How's he been lately?" Tommy asked.

"Better. And worse. And better. The birdwatching helps. The puzzles got boring for him, I guess."

"They would for me, too."

Lola drove back to the main house. Once she cut out of the driver's seat, she wrapped her autumn jacket tighter around her neck and shivered. The second week of October in New England usually hinted toward business. Winter was no joke.

When she entered the living area, she found Susan standing in the center of the room, staring down at the phone in her hand. Her wig was luminescent, stunning, and her lips were parted slightly, as though she had been frozen in place in the middle of a sentence.

Immediately, Lola panicked.

It seemed obvious that Susan had just been on the phone.

"Susan?" Lola whispered, feeling the first bits of panic at her throat. She stood near the counter, in a seemingly perpetual state of dread. "Susan, do you even know I'm here?"

Susan turned her head slowly. She blinked several times and then allowed her phone to fall to the ground.

"Susan, talk to me. Did you get the test results back?" Lola demanded.

Finally, Susan nodded. "I did."

"And?"

"I'm free. Cancer-free. There's nothing else. They got it," she whispered.

Lola burst toward her sister, totally ecstatic, and wrapped her arms around her tightly and held her close. Susan and Lola both sobbed with joy. The sound of it rocketed off the walls and sped up the stairs, incidentally interrupting both Audrey and Wes's naps. Both of them appeared in the living room, groggy, wearing flannel pajamas.

"What's going on?" Audrey asked.

"Cancer! Free!" Susan cried.

Audrey jumped onto her aunt and twirled her around. Wes burst into tears again and wrapped his arms around Susan, holding her head tightly against him—so tight that he accidentally messed up her wig. Susan couldn't have cared less.

"I'll grow a whole new head of hair, anyway!" she said. "It'll be better than ever before."

Chaos ensued after that. Lola supposed that was one of the things she liked most about her family: its affinity for bright lights, color, laughter and too much food, too many opinions, and too many stories to be told. Within minutes, they had decided on a celebration, to be held at the house that very evening. Christine was called to bake a dessert as quickly as she could; when she asked why and received the answer, she all-out screamed into the phone. Lola nearly dropped the it.

"Don't scare Zach and Ronnie," Lola said. "Who, by the way, are both invited. Yes, even Ronnie. Why not? Oh, he has marching band practice. Well, anyway, anyone you want to invite, bring them along! We want the biggest and best Sheridan family party this island has ever seen."

Scott stumbled into the house minutes later and received the news. He fell onto his knees, placed his palms together, and thanked God himself. Susan then crumpled into his arms and kissed him thousands of times on the cheek until his cheeks were red from both embarrassment and happiness and Susan's perfectly tinted lipstick.

"Okay, people!" Susan cried. "This will be our last barbecue of the season. I suggest we also make a bonfire out by the water. That will require wood and lots of it. Audrey? Dad? Maybe the two of you can go hunt for logs."

Audrey saluted. "Aye, aye, captain."

"And the others. Hmm. Lola. Meet Christine at the Inn, grab as many extra snacks as you can from the pantry there—I mean, come on, it's the end of the season, we barely have anyone staying there right now! And then we're going to need burgers and hot dogs and brats and... well. The list goes on and on."

"And the list is always the same," Lola said with a wide grin. "Let's get to work."

Lola burst into the bistro at the Sunrise Cove Inn to find Ronnie leaned against the counter, flicking through his phone, and Zach and Christine baking excitedly and gathering up extra snacks, drinks, and desserts from the pantry.

"Cancer-free!" Zach cried. He lifted a hand, and Lola smacked it.

"I can't believe this," Lola said. "It's over. For real, this time."

"We have to show her a good party," Christine said. "Do you think Amanda has time to make it?"

"No. Not tonight. But I just texted her. She'll come in tomorrow. And she's already made reservations at that wedding dress boutique so that Susan can come with her."

"The Sheridan clan is back on track," Christine stated. "I couldn't be happier."

While Zach finished baking, Christine and Lola headed to the grocery store. They piled their cart with a Christmas celebration's amount of food—so much so that the clerk at the counter arched his brow and said, "You ladies know that summer is over, right?"

"Maybe that's what we're celebrating," Lola said. "Freedom from the tourists."

The guy grumbled and began to scan the articles slowly. "Whatever."

When Zach finished the cake, Lola, Christine, and Zach piled everything into the car and then retreated to the main house again. It was just after six, and guests had begun to arrive in staggered groups. There was Aunt Kerry and Uncle Trevor, all their children and their grandchildren, Susan's best friends, Lily and Sarah, Lola's dear friends, Monica and Hannah, along with all of their families, and Scott's friends, Zach's friends—friends and family members from all walks of life. All wore autumn jackets, some with hats, and they dropped off their beer, wine, and snacks on the main porch before wandering down toward the fire that Audrey, Wes, and Scott had built up together.

There was a lot of hugging—a lot of laughing. Christine, Lola, and Zach dragged various items from the back of the trunk, just as Tommy pulled up in his truck to help out. After hugging and kissing Lola, he greeted Zach with a high-five and congratulated him on some game they had played together.

"Are they hanging out without us?" Lola asked Christine.

"Apparently," Christine said, shrugging.

"I don't know if I like the sound of that," Lola said.

"I think they might get too much power on their own," Christine said, winking back at the guys. "We'll find a way to stop it."

Scott had already begun his long-standing tradition of making enough burgers and hot dogs to feed a small country. Abby and Gail, Claire's fifteen-year-old girls, had begun to show everyone in the living room their newest abilities—juggling three items at once and being able to toss them back and forth, rotating who held which items. Susan lurched in and said, "Be careful, girls! There are some delicate things in here!"

Lola laughed, and Susan stalled. "What?"

"You just sound like the forever Mom. That's all," Lola said.

"What did I say?" Susan asked.

"About breaking things?"

"Oh. I barely know what I say when I say it," Susan said, chuckling. "Hey, do you want to crack open that nice Pinot Grigio Zach talked about? The one you brought from the Inn? I've been dying to try it. Now that the season is over, I think it's time."

Lola agreed and stumbled back through the bags they had brought over to discover it. She cranked the cork out and then poured them each hefty glasses. Christine ambled in from the porch, having apparently escaped from some boring conversation with Uncle Trevor.

"Yes, please," she said with a big smile.

Lola poured another glass.

Together, the three Sheridan sisters walked, wine in-hand, through the party, speaking with as many of their loved ones as they could, snacking and laughing amongst one another. Several times throughout their walk, Scott approached to kiss Susan; Zach approached to tease and dot a kiss on Christine's nose; and Tommy approached with a big bear hug, pretending to take Lola along with him and throw her in the Sound. This, too, ended with a kiss. Each of them faded back into the crowd to converse about sports, about the approaching shift in weather, about how good the fire was. At this, of course, Audrey demanded everyone to tell her just how well-built the fire was. Apparently, she had watched a YouTube video and taught Wes a different way to set up the logs.

Wes lifted his palms to the sky and said, "I've been alive a long time, and I'm still able to learn new things. I have to thank my lucky stars for that."

"Your lucky stars and this Wilderness Man YouTube channel," Audrey added. "But nobody birdwatches like you, Grandpa. You should start a YouTube channel of your own and show everyone the birds of Martha's Vineyard."

Lola paused outside the conversation, turned, and furrowed her brow. "Actually, that's a fantastic idea. Why don't the two of you do that?"

Wes shrugged. "I don't want to deal at all with the technology side of things."

"You won't have to," Audrey insisted. "Just bring that personality and that big head of knowledge, and we'll be good to go."

From the other side of the fire, Audrey gave Lola a slight, meaningful wave. Despite her sass, Lola knew that Audrey was still just a frightened, earnest, whip-smart nineteen-year-old girl, on the verge of something enormous. When she gave birth the following year, everything would change for good. In a way, as she grew closer to her aunts, her grandfather and the island on which they had all grown up, she was allowed a little cozy ecosystem of time, a vacation before the true horror of adulthood began.

Oh, but it wasn't all horror. How could it be? Lola had never been happier in her life. She was borderline-wildly in love with Tommy; she now lived on the most beautiful island on the planet (as far as she was concerned), and, beyond that—she had just been offered a part-time freelance gig at The New York Times.

Lola, Susan, and Christine wandered toward the edge of the dock, kicked off their shoes, and hung their legs down toward the glistening water. The air was chillier by the second. None of the women had anything to say. Their eyes scanned that glorious, orange and pink horizon line, as though they goaded the universe to hit them with something else. They would be ready.

As they sat together, they spotted a tiny fishing boat just out on the yonder waves.

"Is that him?" Lola whispered.

"I think so," Christine returned.

"You didn't invite him, did you?" Susan asked.

"No. But we should have," Lola said. She stood quickly, her heart leaping into her throat, and then waved her hand this way, then that.

Stan Ellis, a man who had been more myth and legend and monster to them than the truth: a man whose life had been destroyed by horror and heartache, slowly turned his head toward the Sheridan residence. After a long pause, he cranked his engine, turned his boat toward them, and motored toward the shore. Orange and pink ripples billowed out behind him.

He returned to where it all began: where the Sheridan clan

would continue to dance and sing and hold one another close, all through that night and a million into the future. His story was intrinsically tied with theirs. He belonged to the strange and varied tapestry of the Sheridan sisters. And it was there, on the Vineyard with them, that he belonged.

CONNECT WITH KATIE WINTERS

Facebook
Amazon
Goodreads
Bookbub

Made in United States
North Haven, CT
01 February 2023

31918514R00136